Stolen Dances and Big City Chances

ALSO BY KATHRYN KALEIGH

Contemporary Romance
The Worthington Family

Stolen Dances and Big City Chances

THE DEVEREAUXS

BELIEVE IN FATE

KATHRYN KALEIGH

STOLEN DANCES AND BIG CITY CHANCES

PREVIEW ACCIDENTALLY FOREVER

Chapter One

ANASTASIA DEVEREAUX

The Sterling House was an iconic old-money Texas-style mansion nestled among flashy skyscrapers in downtown Houston. Texas-style in its 6000 square feet size.

It was decorated for fall which meant bushels of yellow and gold chrysanthemums in vases, tall and small, scattered all around the house.

Tall white pillar candles flickered on the fireplace mantle, the coffee table, and on wall sconces.

The music room was large enough for two elegant chandeliers, lights flickering, one on either side. Above the chandeliers, the ceiling was painted with golden etchings. Below the chandeliers, the polished marble floors reflected the flickering lights.

A lovely young lady in a formal maroon dress sat at the grand piano along with the rest of a four-piece orchestra. Their music echoed through the house.

Silvery sparkling maroon velvet curtains hung at the tall windows with darker burgundy toppers.

It was my brother Austin's wedding day. A beautiful day in the middle of October. A good time to get married in Texas—just after the weather stopped being miserably hot.

Not that he would notice the weather. He didn't see anything other than his bride. Everything was as it should be.

The morning ceremony was followed by a day of celebration before they left for the airport to board a plane for Paris.

I didn't envy him. He was only one year older than me, so we were almost like twins. I was happy for him and I liked his wife, Ava. Austin and Ava had dated in high school, then after going their separate ways for a few years, had taken no time picking up where they had left off. Engaged in December. Married in October.

The Sterling House was crowded with formally dressed men and women, boys and girls. They came for Austin's wedding, but I suspect many also came to see Sterling House.

Our grandparents had built it in another century and lived there until Grandpa had passed away. Grandma hung on, living here for another couple of years by herself, but she missed her family and had moved to Maple Creek to live with her son and daughter-in-law.

Investors had swarmed to buy the property for anything from a parking garage to a shopping mall. She, however, had gone a different direction. She had gotten the house registered with the National Association of Historic Places. Now Austin and Ava's wedding launched what would be a premium venue for weddings and other occasions.

As I walked passed an ornate gilded framed mirror, I almost didn't recognize myself. Recently graduated from college, I hadn't quite given up my wardrobe of jeans and t-shirts.

But today I wore a long chiffon maroon dress. And high heels.

Ava had picked me to be her maid-of-honor. Ava didn't have any family. Our family had been her family since she started dating my brother the first time. Back when they were in high school. I'd missed her during those years when they'd gone their separate ways.

Even now, the happy couple was doing something with cake.

I needed a break.

I stepped outside into the familiar backyard. We'd visited Grandma and Grandpa several times a year back when we were growing up.

It always seemed like the opposite of how most people lived. Most people went to the country to visit their grandparents and lived in the city. We lived in the country and visited our grandparents in the city.

We did all sorts of things in the city. We went to museums, plays, and baseball games. I had a particular fondness for downtown Houston, but I never pictured myself living here.

I preferred the quietness of the country. At least that was my excuse. The truth was, the thought of living alone made me sad.

I loved living with my family. Besides Austin, we had an older brother named Jonathan who was an overseas pilot. Jonathan was about seven years older than me and he only came home on occasions. Like today.

We all knew he was our parents' favorite child. It was okay. We all understood. I always saw Jonathan as being mysterious and interesting. Hard not to favor the mysterious and interesting one.

Then there were our two younger siblings. Theodore and Gwen. They were still in high school. A different generation. Our parents, it seemed, had their children in blocks of two, except for Jonathan. Maybe that was another thing that made him so different.

The maple trees had new green leaves. In fall, those leaves turned a beautiful red. Today in place of the bright red leaves, were tiny red twinkly lights. Someone must have come up with the idea of the red lights in place of the red leaves.

Out here the music sounded different. Faint. Like it was far away. And the conversations were barely audible at all.

If I closed my eyes, I could almost imagine myself back here as a child. When we weren't what Grandma called getting cultured, we played. Playing out here was different from playing at home because out here we were surrounded by skyscrapers.

At night, especially, the skyline around us was awesome. Every time the Astros had a home game, there were fireworks right there where we could watch them from our bedroom windows.

Even now I could hear the sounds of the traffic going up and down the streets. A police car, siren blaring, passed by, heading somewhere fast.

Without the sounds of the city, it would be easy to forget that Sterling House was in the middle of Houston.

It was for sure a different world from Maple Creek where we lived. In Maple Creek, the night sounds consisted of dogs and sometimes wolves howling in the distance. Crickets and owls. Not to mention the silent blinking of the lightning bugs.

There were no lightning bugs in downtown Houston. Not tonight anyway.

My grandmother stepped outside.

"There you are," she said. "I wondered where you got off to."

Grandma was an elegant woman in her sixties. Elegant, but easy to talk to. No one would ever suspect that she lived in a mansion in downtown Houston.

"I just needed to take a moment," I said. "To catch my breath."

"I understand," she said. "It's crowded in there, isn't it?"

"Very," I said.

"You know, Anastasia, weddings are supposed to be a good occasion for you to meet someone."

"Someone?" I asked with a little smile.

"Surely your brother has a nice friend you could spend some time with."

"I'm okay."

A red bird flew past and landed on the birdfeeder in the backyard.

"I thought you brought all the bird feeders when you moved in with us," I said.

"I must have missed one," Grandma said. "I worry about you."

I turned to face my grandmother.

"Why? Why are you worried about me?"

"You're what? Twenty-three?"

"Twenty-four."

"It seems like you should have started dating by now."

I laughed. "I've had dates Grandma."

"Yes. Yes. I know." She looked out across the twinkling lights of the maple trees. "But you should have a boyfriend by now. Someone to start sharing memories with."

Grandma sounded wistful. She and Grandpa had gotten

married when they were barely even legally old enough to marry at all. She had memories with him for probably fifty years.

I didn't want to hurt her feelings by telling her that people didn't do that anymore. That most young people waited until they were in their thirties to get married. By today's standards, I was still young.

Jonathan was thirty and he didn't even have a girlfriend, at least not that I knew of.

Austin was getting married, but he should have married Ava years ago. They had been fated together since they were in seventh grade. They were an anomaly.

The music changed and people were starting to dance.

"Do something for me?" Grandma asked.

"Sure, Grandma. I'll do anything for you."

She linked her arm with mine.

"Let's go back inside. And you." She patted my arm. "You find a nice young man to dance with."

"I don't want to dance, Grandma."

"Just one," she insisted. "Just dance with one young man. I want to see you having some fun."

"I am having fun."

She gave me a look.

"Okay," I said. "I'll see if there is anyone to dance with. But I can't make any promises that there will be anyone."

"Just look," Grandma said. "Looking is a good place to start."

"I'll look," I said, reluctantly.

"Good girl," she said. "Now let's go mingle."

I much preferred my own company, but I didn't want to disappoint my grandmother.

I would go and talk to my brother and his new wife. That was about as close to mingling as I wanted to get right now.

Hopefully, my grandmother would find something else to distract herself with and forget about me and my lack of social interaction.

I did not need a boyfriend right now. My career was just getting started. That was how it was done now. Grandma wouldn't understand.

Chapter Two

CHRISTOPHER Taylor

I wasn't supposed to be at what they were calling the wedding of the season.

One of the pilots who worked for Skye Travels, specifically for Noah Worthington's daughter, was getting married.

Noah Worthington was the founder and owner of Skye Travels, the private airline company he had started with just one little Cessna airplane.

It had grown quickly and was now a multi-billion dollar company. He hired his own family without shame. The only thing was they had to do in order to get hired was to be better than anyone else.

Since I was in no way, shape, or form related to the Worthington family, I considered myself fortunate to land a job flying for Skye Travels.

I was the only one in my graduating class fortunate to be hired by Noah Worthington. And I literally was hired by Noah himself. He might be getting up in age, but he still personally interviews every single pilot who goes to work for his company.

At any rate, I was the newest hire at Skye Travels and my mentor asked me to come along since his girlfriend was out of town.

I was hardly in a position to tell him I couldn't go. Not when I was just starting a brand new job.

So that's how I found myself at Sterling House, wearing a rented tuxedo, feeling exceptionally uncomfortable around hundreds of people I did not know, most of whom I would never see again.

I was just a regular guy—a pilot. I didn't attend fundraisers or other soirees unless I went as a client's guest. So I chalked today up to a work function.

The Sterling House was on the National Register of Historical places or some such. It belonged to Austin Devereaux's grandmother.

I'd lived in Houston my whole life, but I'd only been downtown a handful of times and I certainly didn't know that there was a mansion nestled right downtown among the high rises.

Like the other pilots, I drank a sparkling water in lieu of alcohol. I had a flight tomorrow and Noah Worthington had a very strict bottle to throttle policy.

One drink would get a pilot a warning. Two would get him suspended. And three would get him a trip to rehab. Or so I had been told.

I had a feeling getting fired was somewhere in there, especially for new guys.

So I stuck to sparkling water and no one thought a thing about it.

The little orchestra was set up in the music room, their music light and airy. It was happy music for a happy day.

"Come on," Frederick, my mentor said. "I'll introduce you to Austin."

Frederick had been a pilot for Skye Travels for right at eight years. He knew his way around the family and a fancy wedding at a fancy house didn't intimidate him one bit, even if he was more like me than he might want to admit.

Frederick was what I would call a flashy guy. He always wore a flirty smile, especially when he was around the ladies and he walked with what could only be called a swagger. A pilot's swagger.

Even now as we walked across the ballroom, he attracted attention. Every single female we passed checked him out. I kept track.

It wasn't that I cared. I was not a playboy. I'd had a couple of girlfriends, but I didn't date around. I didn't have a girl in every port or anything like I happened to know that Frederick did.

To each his own.

Although we were different in that way, we were alike in other ways. Like me, Frederick was an uptown boy. Uptown was by far a rougher area than downtown. The opposite was nothing more than a misperception.

"I think I met Austin once," I said, but I went along anyway.

"You can meet his new wife then," Frederick said, making his way through the crowd. We had to move carefully because people were dancing now. Waltzing to be exact.

Waltzing was most definitely outside of my purview.

Austin and his new wife were sitting together eating cake and laughing with each other. Now that was something I envied. My sister was married. They had one little girl—wrapped around my little finger—and another on the way.

That was the kind of lifestyle I wanted to lead.

As we neared the happy couple, a dark-haired goddess wearing a maroon dress came up and sat down right behind them. Her long flowing hair framed a heart-shaped face with red bow-shaped lips.

Frederick stopped in front of the couple and put a hand over his heart.

"Ava," he said. "You've gone and broken my heart."

Ava, apparently Austin's wife, just smiled.

"I have a feeling you'll bounce back just fine," Ava said.

"Go find your own girl, Frederick," Austin said with nothing but harmless amusement. "This one is mine."

"Fine. Fine. But first you need to meet Christopher Taylor. He's the newest Skye Travels pilot."

"Try not to pick up Frederick's bad habits," Ava said. "He will get you in trouble."

The dark haired goddess sitting behind them was watching Frederick in that way that women did. Like they couldn't take their eyes off of him.

Personally, if I was a girl, I would be turned off by his muscles. I was lean and in shape, but my muscles weren't cut. I didn't care to look sculpted. Flying was my gig.

"Nice to meet you both," I said. "And congratulations on your marriage."

"Are you from Houston?" Ava asked me.

The goddess sitting behind them leaned forward and whispered something to Austin.

"Yes," I said. "Uptown. Nothing like this."

Austin was shaking his head at the goddess.

"No," he said. "Not a good idea."

She whispered something else to him.

"Nothing wrong with Uptown," Ava said. "Have a sparkling water and enjoy yourself."

"I will. Thank you." I held up my glass of sparkling water and took note of the champagne glass in her hand. Austin was holding a glass of champagne, too. He wouldn't be doing any flying tomorrow, not as the pilot, at any rate.

"Don't say I didn't warn you," Austin told the girl sitting behind him, frowning.

"Frederick," he said. "This is my sister, Anastasia."

Frederick's face lit up like he'd just been given the keys to a brand new Phenom.

"Anastasia. What a beautiful name. For a beautiful lady. It's a pleasure to meet you." He held out a hand, but instead of shaking her hand, he brought it to his lips and kissed her palm.

I refrained from rolling my eyes, but barely.

Austin must have seen the struggle I was having. We exchanged a knowing look.

So the dark-haired beauty was Austin's sister. Anastasia.

And Anastasia had just been introduced to the biggest womanizer I had ever known.

Before I even caught onto what was going on, Frederick and Anastasia were headed out onto the dance floor where he pulled her into a waltz.

They looked good together. I had to give them that. But they were both pretty people in their own right. There was no way they couldn't look good together.

"What was that about?" Ava asked her husband.

"Something about Grandma," Austin said, keeping his gaze on his sister a moment longer.

"Well," Ava said. "I don't understand that."

"Unfortunately, I can't watch out for her," Austin said, cupping his wife's chin and placing a kiss on her lips. "It's my wedding day."

She smiled, then looked over at me.

"Good point. But maybe Christopher could look out for her."

"Whoa," I said, holding up a hand. "Frederick does what Frederick does. No offense to your sister."

"None taken," Austin said. "I'm far too familiar with Frederick."

"You have to do something," Ava said. "You can't just introduce them and not watch out for her."

"Anastasia is a grown woman," Austin said, then turned back to me. "Can you watch out for her? Just today. After that you're off the hook."

I hadn't known that going to a man's wedding meant I would have to watch out for his sister. That seemed like a task far beyond the call of duty.

"I'll do my best," I said.

What was a man supposed to do?

Offend a man at his wedding? Probably not a good idea.

Refuse to keep an eye on his beautiful goddess of a sister? Not a chance.

"Thank you," Austin said. "I owe you one."

"No problem."

"Nice to meet you," Ava said before Austin tipped her back in another kiss.

Looked to me like the two of them were far beyond ready to get started on the honeymoon.

Unsure what I was supposed to do now. What I was really supposed to do... I wandered over to the open bar and got myself a fresh glass of sparkling water.

Then I leaned back against the bar and watched the dancers until I caught sight of Frederick whirling Anastasia around the room. They weren't hard to locate. Not with her in her red dress.

"Excuse me," an older man, said as he came up to the bar. I stepped aside and looked around for another place to station myself with my unsolicited task.

I was beginning to see the value in learning to waltz. Maybe I'd check into lessons. Not that I would have all that many opportunities to waltz. Not in the ordinary world I lived in.

Still. It couldn't hurt. Working for the Worthington family, I never knew what I might be called up to do.

"Thank you Mr. Worthington," the bartender said. "Enjoy."

I hadn't recognized him at first, but that was THE Noah Worthington. Noah was a distinguished looking older man. He might have gray hair, but it only made him look all the more distinguished. A man could only aspire to be as successful as Noah Worthington and to remain as handsome with age.

Noah stood next to me. I couldn't tell if he was drinking champagne or sparkling water or maybe something else entirely.

"How are you Christopher?" he asked.

"Fine, Sir," I said. "A beautiful wedding."

"Those two should have been married years ago." He straightened. Gave a little shake of his head. "A familiar tale."

"How so?" I asked.

"I made the same mistake with Savannah. Got lucky when she took me back, though God only knows why she did."

"It was meant to be, Sir," I said.

He rocked back on his heels. "Can't argue with that."

"Is Ms. Worthington here?" I asked.

"Yes," he said. "Excuse my bad manners. Come on. I'll introduce you."

"You don't have to—"

But Noah was already walking away, obviously assuming I would follow.

He was a man who expected men to follow him and they did. I'd yet to meet anyone who didn't admire Noah Worthington or an employee who wasn't loyal to him.

I had met a few people who were envious of him, but none who wished him ill. I'm sure they were out there—there was always someone—but I never let a conversation go down that direction. I hadn't worked for him long, but I had, it seemed, already fallen into that loyalist camp.

He was charmed as far as I could figure.

Any man who could take one little Cessna airplane and turn it into a billion dollar company was the epitome of success, definitely admired by pilots all across the country.

I followed Noah through the crowded ballroom, past half a dozen men who greeted him. Past dancers on the ballroom floor.

As instructed, I kept one eye on Anastasia as Frederick swept her around the dance floor.

Noah stopped in front of two beautiful women, one clearly older than the other. They stood, their heads bent together, deep in conversation, but as we approached, the older woman looked up and smiled at Noah.

He kissed her on the cheek in a show of affection, most men of his station wouldn't dare in this type of formal setting.

"Savannah," he said. "This is Christopher Taylor. He's one of our newest pilots."

"It's a pleasure to meet you, Christopher," she said. "Welcome to the team."

"It's an honor, ma'am."

Savannah turned to the woman standing next to her.

"This is our daughter Ainsley. She runs our animal transport department."

"Hello Christopher," Ainsley said. Ainsley was tall like her father and had her mother's features. She looked as good as expected, coming from two good-looking successful parents.

"Be careful," Savannah said. "She'll try to recruit you."

"As long as it involves flying," I said.

Noah clapped me on the back.

"Spoken like a true pilot," he said.

"You have to love animals," she said. "It's a lot different from flying human passengers."

"I can only imagine."

I caught a glimpse of red as Anastasia swept past in Frederick's arms.

I couldn't help but watch them as they passed. It was my job, after all.

"We've got to do something about that," Ainsley said.

"Ainsley," Savannah said. "It's not our business."

I couldn't pretend to know what they were talking about. It sounded like they were talking about Anastasia, but I had no way of knowing if that was a correct assumption.

"Are you two still talking about Anastasia?" Noah asked, verifying my suspicions.

"It's our duty," Ainsley said.

"It's not our business," Savannah insisted.

"Anastasia Devereaux is the granddaughter of the owner of this building—The Sterling House," Noah told me.

"Austin's brother."

"Yes," Noah said. "You know her?"

"I can't say that I do, but..." How much did I want to disclose? This was my boss. I had no reason to hide anything from him. "But Austin asked me to look after her tonight."

"See," Ainsley said. "Even Austin is worried about her."

"He did seem worried about her," I said. "But it's his wedding day..."

"It's Frederick," Ainsley said. "Everyone knows he can't be trusted around women."

They were all three looking at me now. Noah, Savannah, and their daughter Ainsley.

"You've got to break in there," Ainsley said.

"Break in there? What does that mean?" A sense of panic was settling into my stomach and I was beginning to regret coming here tonight.

"She means cut in," Noah said, then added at my blank expression. "Cut in and dance with her."

Now I really was going to be sick.

"Sorry, Sir. I don't dance."

"Everyone dances," Ainsley said, dismissively.

"Ainsley," Savannah said with the tone only a mother could use.

"Just walk up there, tap Frederick on the shoulder, and take his place. He has to give her up."

"Do people still do that?" Savannah wondered, looking over at her husband.

Noah glanced around the room at the dancers.

"It might be a little old-fashioned."

"It might be very old-fashioned."

"Who cares?" Ainsley said. "We can't stand by and let Rebecca Devereaux's granddaughter's reputation be destroyed."

She had a good point, but I didn't see how sending me in was going to change that. Anastasia might not even want to dance with me. As far as I could tell, she appeared to be having a good time with Frederick.

Not surprising. Frederick had a way with women that I would never understand.

"Daddy if he won't do it," Ainsley said. "You will."

Noah looked at his daughter. Shook his head.

"And that would look how?" he asked.

"I told you it's not our business," Savannah said. "Anastasia is a grown woman."

Ainsley put her hands on her hips and glared at no one in particular.

Then she turned her gaze back to me.

"You have to do it," she said. "It's Austin's sister."

I was shaking my head.

No matter how much regret I was having right now, it was too late to take dance lessons now.

I'd been tossed into the deep end by the Worthington family.

I had more than a feeling that no one told them no.

I could be the first.

Chapter Three

ANASTASIA

I was only dancing with Frederick to make my grandmother happy.

It was just a side benefit that all the other women at my brother's wedding gave me envious glances as he swept me around the ballroom.

Just a side benefit.

And Frederick had smooth moves. The way he looked at me like I was the only woman here tonight was a heady feeling.

But it was only to make my grandmother happy.

I caught a glimpse of her as we swirled past. She should have been smiling. I was, after all, only doing what she'd asked me to do.

She'd asked me to find someone and dance with them. Just one dance, she'd said.

I was already into my third dance with Frederick and right about now, to be quite honest, I could use a glass of cold water.

But Grandma wasn't smiling. She was talking quite seriously with a woman I recognized as Savannah Worthington. Savannah Worthington was Noah's wife. Noah Worthington. The owner and founder of Skye Travels. My brother's boss.

Why would they be talking? And why did they keep glancing in my direction?

I realized, a bit belatedly, that Frederick had asked me something.

He'd already asked me three "Would you rather" questions. None of them had answers that made any sense and I was quite honestly getting weary of them.

"I'm sorry," I said. "I didn't quite catch that." It was easy to blame the music and conversations swirling around us for my lack of attention.

"Would you rather be able to shrink down to the size of an ant or to grow to the size of a skyscraper?"

"Excuse me?"

Frederick laughed and repeated his question.

"I don't know," I said. "A skyscraper, I guess."

"Why?" He deftly swept me past a pair of dancers, people I didn't recognize.

"So I could see a long way off I guess."

"I'd rather be able to shrink down like an ant," Frederick said.

"Why?" I asked, but the whole question made no sense to me.

"So I could slide into someone's pocket and listen in on their conversations."

"That sounds rather underhanded."

He looked a little offended. How could he be offended by that? He'd started the whole ridiculous conversation.

"I'd like to stop," I said. "For a glass of water."

"Sure. We should finish out this dance though."

"I really don't—"

We turned and someone tapped Frederick on the shoulder.

Thank God. Someone was cutting in.

"What?" Frederick asked.

"I'm cutting in," the man said.

I recognized the man as the one who had been introduced by Frederick as Christopher.

"You can't just—"

"Actually," I said. "He can."

I somehow removed my hand from Frederick's arm and put it on Christopher's. Not an easy move while we were dancing.

"Whatever," Frederick said, with obvious annoyance, letting me go.

As he walked away, Christopher and I stood still, my heart racing from all the dancing.

"Thank you," I told Christopher. "Can we just get something to drink? A glass of water?"

"A glass of water?" Christopher asked. We were standing in the middle of the dance floor now, neither one of us moving. "We can most definitely get a glass of water."

I was so thirsty, I thought I imagined the look of relief on his face.

He tucked my hand in the crook of his arm and led me off the dance floor toward the bar.

As we passed my grandmother and Mrs. Worthington, they both smiled at us.

"I'm Christopher," he as we took our place in line at the open bar.

"I know. I'm Anastasia."

"I know," he said. "You're Austin's sister."

I nodded. Considered.

"What made you come to my rescue?" I asked.

"Did I? Come to your rescue?" he asked. "You seemed to be having a good time with Frederick."

"Thirsty," I said to myself. "I needed a break."

"I see."

We reached the bar.

"Two glasses of ice water," he said.

The bartender slid over one glass, then another.

I took mine. Drained it.

"Can we get a refill?" Christopher asked.

"Sure thing." The bartender refilled my glass and handed me a cold bottle of water to go with my glass of water.

"Thank you," I said.

"Let's find a place to sit down."

"Yes. Let's." Sweeping my hair back off my neck, I followed Christopher to a sofa in the study next to the ballroom. I felt like I had just finished a cardio workout.

After we settled onto the sofa, I opened my bottle of water and filled my glass again.

"I think I made Frederick mad," I said.

"I wouldn't worry about him if I were you," he said.

"Why not?"

He nodded toward the door. Frederick was walking outside with a woman I didn't recognize.

"Well," I said, looking away.

"Do you mind?"

I shrugged. "I just met him. Doesn't do much for my ego though."

"Your ego doesn't need him."

I looked over at him sideways. "You're friends with him, right?"

"Frederick is my work mentor. So friends? Not so much."

"Good." I poured the rest of my water into my glass, the cool water sparkling over the ice cubes.

"Can I get you some more water?" he asked.

"Maybe in a few minutes. I'm okay for now."

"Just let me know."

"How do you know Austin?"

"I just met him."

"Ava?" Ava didn't have any family, but she did have friends, mostly work friends.

"Just me her, too."

"You just came with Frederick."

"That's right," he said.

"What made you cut in?"

"It's a long story," he said. "I'll tell you after we get to know each other better."

I smiled and although it was a simple statement that probably meant nothing at all, it was simple statement that gave me butterflies.

It was a simple declaration that he wanted to get to know me better. Somehow that pleased me.

My grandmother had insisted that I dance with someone. I'd almost ignored it, but I really would do anything for my grandmother.

When Frederick showed up, seeming to know both my brother and his wife, I'd called in a favor. One of many favors my brother owed me.

I should have heeded his warning about Frederick, but the way Frederick kept glancing at me told me that he would be willing to dance with me. It would make my grandmother happy.

How was I supposed to know that once we started dancing he wasn't going to let me go? I wasn't sure which was worse. That he wouldn't let me go or that he kept asking me stupid "what if" questions.

"Can I ask you something?" Christopher asked.

"Please don't ask me a what if question."

"Okay. I won't." He took a sip of water and frowned at me. "I don't really know what that is."

"Then yes." I smiled over at him. "In that case, you can ask me a question."

"How is it you're the most beautiful girl here tonight?"

"You can't ask me that," I said, leaning toward him, keeping my voice low.

"Why not? Is it a what if question?"

"No." I laughed. "You can't because it's Ava's wedding."

"Oh. Well. I wasn't counting her. That's a given."

I smiled. My grandmother just might have been right after all.

Maybe it didn't hurt to meet someone to spend a little with after all.

Chapter Four

CHRISTOPHER

It was a well-accepted fact in some circles that when a man met the woman he wanted to spend his life with he knew it immediately.

Although I had no reason to either believe it or not believe it up until now, I was quickly becoming a believer.

Anastasia was absolutely enchanting.

I'd known it the moment I first saw her. When she sat near her brother and his wife and got her brother to introduce her to Frederick.

Music befitting a wedding, sometimes happy and sometimes heartbreakingly romantic, swirled through the air. It blended with laughter and conversations.

Three photographers roamed the house, someone always staying focused on the newlyweds. They were going to have thousands of pictures to choose from. I did not envy them that.

"Why Frederick?" I asked.

Anastasia took a deep breath. Shook her head a little.

"It's a long story," she said repeating my words back to me. "I'll tell you after we get to know each other better."

I laughed. "Deal. You know. I don't think I've ever been to a morning wedding before."

"My brother had to be different. Actually they're flying to Paris tonight. I think. Their flight got rescheduled and they already had the wedding planned."

"That explains it," I said. "One of my friends in college had a wedding party that lasted two days."

"That seems a little extravagant to me," she said. "Seems like a wedding is something to do and get on with it. Small and quick."

She really was a woman after my heart.

"I couldn't agree more."

"You're not into big weddings?" she asked.

"I don't think I'm suited to big weddings."

"Why not?" She set her glass down on the end table and pulled her hair loose around over one shoulder.

"It's not something I should tell you," I said.

"Well. Now you have to tell me."

"That's how it works, isn't it?"

She gave me a little smile. "Of course it is."

"It's not a secret, so I guess I might as well tell you."

She leaned forward, one eyebrow raised.

"You've got me imagining all sorts of things," she said.

"I don't know how to waltz." There. I'd told her. It had to be told even if it meant she never spoke to me again.

She looked blankly at me as though trying to comprehend.

"Is that it?" she asked.

"That's it."

"That's not a good reason, you know."

I waved a hand in the direction of the ballroom. "Seems like a pretty good reason to me."

"It's fixable," she said. "People take lessons all the time."

"I'm going to have to look into that."

We sat in silence a few minutes while the music changed again. This time it was back to a romantic tune, but with a happy beat to it.

"But you cut in. You were going to dance with me."

"That's part of that long story I'll be telling you in a few years."

"A few years," she said on a little laugh.

"Yeah... Maybe. If then."

"Well. I won't let you forget," she said with a little smile that lit up her enchanting big green eyes. The way she was smiling at me made her eyes look like a green forest after a rain.

"No," I said, unable to look away from her. "I wouldn't think you would."

I figured I had a definite advantage as far as her memory went. I would always be the guy she met at her brother's wedding.

And as for me... She would always be the girl I fell in love with at first sight.

Chapter Five

Anastasia

The rest of the afternoon was taken up with formal photographs and toasts and stories and more food.

I was summoned over to spend what seemed like forever taking photos with my family. Then we all had to go outside for evening photographs.

Seriously, I couldn't imagine what Austin and Ava were going to do with so many thousands of photographs and videos.

There was the tossing of the bouquet which I did not, thankfully, come anywhere near to catching. I didn't need that added pressure. I was the oldest girl in the family and with Austin married, my mother was going to start looking at me any day now. Asking me about my wedding plans.

I had no wedding plans and I was quite happy with that.

Darkness fell early and brought chilly air with it.

There was staff hired to go around and turn up each one of the five fireplaces downstairs alone. Upstairs where there were three or four more fireplaces was restricted to family only.

It was getting close to time for Austin and Ava to head out to the airport.

Even knowing it was their honeymoon and they were happy, I felt a little sad about it. I think part of that was the fact that with my closest brother getting married, nothing would ever be quite the same again.

Just before it was time for them to leave, we were all summoned out back.

Surely we weren't going to be required to pose for more pictures. But Austin and Ava had changed into their travel clothes. A regular suit for Austin and a pencil skirt and matching jacket for Ava. They looked so cute and so ready for their honeymoon.

I swear I wasn't jealous of them. I just felt a little envious. I was content to be single and no designs on marriage anytime in the future, but they were a picture of what could be.

But it wasn't just family summoned outside. It was everyone.

I'd only seen Christopher in passing for the last couple of hours, but as we headed out back, he caught up with me and walked alongside me.

"Hi," he said.

"Hi."

"What is this about?" he asked.

"I don't know," I said as we stepped outside and made our way to the flower garden area where everyone was gathering.

Tall colorful snapdragons were a background layer for blue

plumbagos and yellow orange chrysanthemums. The stone path through the flower garden was lined with white wooden benches which at the moment were filled with older guests.

"You're supposed to know," Christopher said. "You're the sister."

"You would think so," I agreed. "I'd say I need to have a word with my brother, but I'm sure even he knows what's going on."

We both looked over at Austin and Ava, standing together, focusing on each other, not seeming to care in the least what else was going on. They were getting ready to spend two weeks alone. Just them. No one else. No family around to influence what they did.

That in itself was unusual for our close-knit family.

"I have a feeling he doesn't really care," Christopher said.

"Yeah. I feel a little embarrassed for them right now."

"I think they look happy. I'm happy for them."

I looked over at Christopher. "Do you have any brothers or sisters?"

"I have a sister," he said. "Married. One child and one on the way."

"Hmm. I guess you're used to all this then."

"I wouldn't say I'm used to it. She got married about... five years ago."

"She's older?"

"Four years older."

Everyone was looking around, waiting for whatever it was we were supposed to be doing outside.

"What do you think they're up to?" Christopher asked.

"I can't even begin to imagine."

It was only a few minutes later when we found out just why we had been summoned outside in the darkness.

Fireworks.

Lots of fireworks.

They shot high into the sky and exploded into pops of red and gold. Big explosions mixed with smaller bursts of color.

Christopher stood close and our hands brushed as we watched the fireworks.

About halfway through, his pinky linked loosely with mine.

The light, casual, yet oddly intimate touch had my blood racing through my veins.

I hadn't expected to meet someone that I actually liked at my brother's wedding.

I had expected to make my grandmother happy by dancing with someone. That was it.

But instead, I had met Christopher.

A pilot. Just like both my older brothers. Mostly like Austin who also flew private planes for Skye Travels. Jonathan was a different kind of pilot.

He flew the kind of big commercial jets that Austin and Ava were going to take on their trip to Paris.

Jonathan was rarely home. Unlike Austin who only occasionally had to stay gone on overnight trips.

That meant that Christopher would be home most nights. For some reason, that pleased me. I had no reason to be pleased by it. I'd probably never even see him again after today or if I did, I'd probably see him in passing at a function similar to this.

And that thought made me inordinately sad. It was odd because I didn't really date and didn't really have any interest in it.

But somehow Christopher had snagged my attention and I wanted to spend more time with him. I wanted to get to know him better.

But we were what they called a wedding romance. Sort of like a summer romance, but shorter. Summer romances, at least had a three month span of possibilities.

Wedding romances typically had one night.

After the fireworks ended, Christopher released my hand and we all clapped.

"We'll see you all later," Austin said with a big wave, grabbing his wife's hand, and together the two of them slipped out to catch their ride to the airport.

After they left, everyone was quiet.

No one seemed to know what to do.

"Let's all head back inside," my father announced. "It's time for the real party to start now."

As we all made our way back inside, Christopher took my hand and led me back to the study where we had sat earlier.

"Are you okay?" he asked.

"Of course," I said, sitting down on the sofa. "Why do you ask?"

He swept a finger lightly across my cheek and came back with moisture.

"Oh," I said, wiping at my cheeks. I hadn't even realized that I was crying. But now that I thought about it, my throat did feel tight.

"You like Ava, right?"

"I like Ava a lot."

"Look at it this way," Christopher said. "You're gaining a new sister. Your brother is happy. And if you're lucky, you'll be an aunt before you know it."

"That sounds promising," I said with a little smile. "I hadn't considered that I might be an aunt."

"There's nothing like it," he said. "Well. I mean there's nothing like being an uncle, so I have to assume that there is nothing like being an aunt either."

"You really like your sister's child, huh?"

"A little girl. Her name is Lily."

"That's a pretty name."

"She's adorable. I'll introduce you to her."

"Is that allowed?"

"Why wouldn't it be?"

"Aren't you supposed wait until it's serious to introduce a child to... someone?"

"Well, first of all, I'm not her father, so that rule doesn't apply. And second, who says it isn't serious?"

I nodded slowly, not knowing how to respond to that.

All I could think was that Christopher saw things differently than most people because he was a pilot.

From the stories Austin told me, pilots had a unique way of looking at the world. The world for a pilot was smaller. Less mysterious.

They could hop on an airplane and be in another city in another state in the time it took us mere mortals to drive across Houston.

It definitely changed a person's perspective.

"Don't look so troubled," Christopher said. "You'll like my sister and you'll love Lily."

"Okay." I smiled. "When do I get to meet them?"

He leaned back. "How about tomorrow?"

"Tomorrow?" Surely he wasn't serious.

"Sure. We always try to get together on Sunday afternoons."

"Really? My family does that, too. But probably not tomorrow. Everyone will be recovering from the wedding."

"Sounds perfect then," he said. "You'll get to spend some time with my family without neglecting yours."

I was having trouble thinking of a reason to say no. I felt like I should say no.

It all seemed so sudden. And so intense.

But I was coming up empty-handed.

Not only could I not come up with a reason to say no, I was quickly realizing that I didn't want to say no.

"Okay," I said. "I'll be staying here tonight. Where does your sister live? I can meet you there."

"You can't meet me there," he said. "But I can pick you up."

Chapter Six

CHRISTOPHER

There were most definitely benefits to only drinking nothing stronger than sparkling water at a wedding.

I woke the next morning with a clear head along with a sense of anticipation. There were a whole lot of people who'd been at the wedding who woke up this morning with headaches.

It didn't matter that I hadn't met Austin and Ava before last night. Their wedding was a game changer for me.

Had me looking at things a whole lot differently.

I'd been going along quite contentedly with my life. Dating now and then, nothing serious. Mostly I went out with girls who pursued me.

Mary Beth was the last girl I'd fallen for at first sight like this.

Mary Beth and I been six-years-old at the time. She'd moved

away the next year and I didn't even know where she was now. Hadn't known since then. But her memory lingered and left me knowing that feeling of falling head over heels.

I had that feeling with Anastasia. Stronger even. Anastasia was, after all, a grown woman and I was taking her home to meet my family.

They didn't know I was bringing her. They'd find out when we got there.

As I pulled up to the Sterling House, there was a guard and a valet on staff.

Apparently they were expecting me. I was instructed to park over to the side and go on in.

Interesting.

When I stepped inside the front door, into the foyer, I was quite taken off-guard.

It was nine o'clock the morning after a large, moderately extravagant wedding.

And yet there was no indication whatsoever that there had been a wedding here. Everything was picked up and it looked as though the wedding had never even happened.

I stood in front of the tall grandfather clock watching the swinging pendulum, idly wondering if I was in the right place.

Since I was pretty sure this was the only mansion in the middle of downtown Houston, I had little doubt that I was in the right place.

Although the driveway was heavily guarded, there was no one inside to give me any guidance as to where I should go now that I was inside.

So I just stood in the foyer and waited patiently.

My patience lasted about thirty seconds before I started pacing back and forth.

Turning, my hands behind my back, I looked toward the grand staircase. The velvet rope with "Do Not Enter" had been removed.

It was a little hard to believe that Anastasia's grandmother had lived here in this mansion and Anastasia had visited often. It looked like a house out of a magazine, not the kind of house people actually lived in.

She didn't seem to think it was anything unusual.

My condo would fit inside the ballroom alone.

When Anastasia appeared at the top of the steps, all thoughts of Sterling House left my brain.

She'd been beautiful yesterday dressed in her maid-of-honor dress. Very elegant looking. Today she was dressed in a flowy skirt with a warm sweater and looked just adorable and at ease.

She smiled when she saw me, before she started down the stairs.

"You look beautiful," I said as she neared the bottom stairs.

"You're looking rather handsome yourself," she said as her feet touched the floor.

I fought the urge to pick her up and twirl her around.

I might not know how to dance a waltz, but I knew how to pick up a girl and spin her around in my arms.

But I was good. Instead, I leaned over and kissed her on the forehead.

"Are you ready to go?" I asked.

"Ready," she said, holding up the strap around her shoulders that held her phone.

"We're off then," I said.

"You still haven't told me where we're going."

"It's a surprise," I said. I hadn't told her. I think I was afraid that if I told her, she wouldn't go.

"You're driving?"

It seemed like a rather odd question.

"I have a rental."

"Okay," she said and we walked outside together.

She greeted the valet and the guard before I opened the passenger door and she climbed in.

As I went around to the driver's side I couldn't shake the feeling that I was missing something.

Chapter Seven

ANASTASIA

Christopher hadn't told me where his sister lived. He'd insisted it was a surprise.

It didn't take me long to figure out that she lived north of Houston.

"This is the way I go home," I said. "Does your sister live in Maple Creek?"

"Where?"

"Maple Creek. It's a tiny little town north of Houston."

"You still live there?" he asked, glancing over at me as he navigated traffic.

"Yes. With my parents and two younger siblings. Before last night, Austin lived there, too."

"You drive in to Houston for work?"

"I actually work from home."

When he didn't say anything, I filled in some of the gaps for him.

"I'm a grant writer for a nonprofit. I drive into the office in Houston about once every other week."

"We have completely different lifestyles," he said. "Sometimes it feels like I'm only home every other week."

I nodded and looked away. Watched the traffic flowing past on the familiar freeway.

It seemed odd that he was telling me this.

Last night, I'd been thinking how he was probably home every night. Like my brother.

"Austin is almost always home at night," I said.

"He works for Ainsley though, right? Pet transport?"

"That's true. I guess that's a little different."

"I never know what my schedule is going to be from one week to the next."

He exited off the freeway and headed toward the airport.

"Do you like working for Skye Travels?" I asked.

"Best job I could imagine having."

"Austin likes it, too."

Was he trying to warn me that he was gone away from home a lot? I couldn't quite figure out why he was telling me that he spent a lot of time traveling.

I liked it better before I knew that.

Knowing that he was rarely home left me feeling... disappointed.

I'd heard Austin talk about pilots and how the more they traveled the more girlfriends they had.

According to Austin, the pilot's lifestyle was a well-known fact.

I had a feeling things weren't going to work out with Christopher.

Like he said, he and I had completely different lifestyles.

"Your sister lives near the airport?" I asked as he turned down the road leading to the airport.

"Something like that," he said with a grin.

I gave him a look as he turned into the Skye Travels parking lot.

"Is this the surprise?" I asked.

"Yes." He turned off the motor. "I'll come around and open the door."

This was not at all what I was expecting.

When he opened the door, I stepped out.

"We're going flying?" I asked. "I thought we were going to visit your sister."

"We are," he said with a grin. "She lives near Denver."

"Denver?" I didn't follow when he started to take a step forward. "You didn't tell me that."

"It's a surprise," he said.

"Does she know I'm coming?"

"I haven't told her that."

"No," I said. "I don't think this is a good idea."

He looked out toward the runway where a small jet was taking off.

After studying me for a moment, he pulled out his cell phone and tapped on the screen to make a call.

"Hey Char," he said. "You're on speaker."

"Hey Christopher," Char said. "Where are you? Lily keeps asking me when you're going to be here."

"I'm just leaving Houston. But I have a quick question for you."

"Okay. What's up?"

"Do you mind if I bring a guest?"

"Why would I mind? You know I don't."

He held out the phone.

"Tell Anastasia that."

"Hi," I said, not knowing what else to say.

"Hi. Is my brother behaving himself?"

"He's a perfect gentleman." I looked into Christopher's smiling blue eyes.

"He better be. I'm not sure why he's asking me. He's always welcome to bring a guest even if it is unusual."

"I didn't know you lived in Denver."

"Oh. Christopher is a good pilot. I've let him take my daughter up if that tells you anything."

"It does. Thank you."

"Great. I'll see you in a few hours then."

"Okay," I said, at a loss for anything else to say.

Christopher took the phone back.

"Thanks Char. See you shortly."

Austin was right. Pilots had a different view of the way the world worked.

He was telling his sister he would see her shortly when we had a flight ahead of us.

Maybe to him flying to Denver really was no different from driving across Houston to Katy.

Now his sister was expecting me.

If I didn't go, I would look bad and make him look bad.

I'd been raised better than that.

Looked like I was going to Denver today.

Chapter Eight

CHRISTOPHER

The scent of jet fuel on the runway was one of those comforting scents. For me, at least. That and the sound of jet engines landing and taking off.

The private Skye Travels airport terminal had become like a familiar second home to me. I felt more at ease here, in fact, than I did in my own condo.

I automatically glanced over at the wind sock. No wind today. A good day for a flight.

I'd messed up with Anastasia.

I could see that now.

It was just another indication that I didn't date often enough.

I should have told her we were going flying.

I went flying every day. It wasn't a big deal to me. I should have thought how it might seem to Anastasia.

That it would be a big deal.

Not just going to visit my sister and her family on a whim, but flying from Houston to Denver to do it.

Anastasia was different from most girls. First of all her brother was a pilot. I think that fact was what got me confused to begin with. For some reason, I seemed to think that since her brother was a pilot, she would be used to flying.

Pilots were well known for hopping in a plane on a whim, flying somewhere for a hamburger or a shrimp po'boy, then flying right back where they started.

For the love of the flight.

But the point was her brother was a pilot. She wasn't. Anastasia worked from home, so she rarely went anywhere.

And second of all, she was just different.

She was the kind of girl I wanted to marry.

Hell. Who was I trying to fool? She was THE girl I wanted to marry.

I hadn't felt this way about anyone since Mary Beth in kindergarten. Twenty-five years ago. Good God. It had been twenty-five years since I had felt this way about a girl.

Anastasia was special and she was the kind of girl a man should cherish.

So I had learned my lesson. No more surprises.

As I waited for the stairs on the plane to lower to the ground, I told her so.

"No more surprises," I said.

"You promise?" she asked, squinting at me in the bright sunlight.

"Yes."

"I can't see your eyes," she said.

I immediately dragged my sun glasses off and placed them over her eyes.

Now I couldn't see her eyes, but I looked right at her.

"No more surprises," I said. "Unless you like surprises, which I don't think you do."

"I might like surprises sometimes," she said. "After I've known you for a few years."

"Fair enough," I said. And a good answer. Relief flooded through me. If she was thinking in any way shape or form of us several years from now, then all was not lost.

She went up the stairs first and waited for me.

"Where do I sit?" she asked.

"In the copilot's seat," I said, leading the way to the cockpit.

"I've never been a copilot," she said, taking a seat.

"Austin never let you fly with him?"

"I've been flying, but not as the copilot. He made us all sit in the cabin."

"Huh. Then I guess you're going to need help with this harness."

"Probably," she said, looking down at the complicated four-point harness.

"Let me help you out with that," I said, leaning over and taking both end of the harness to snap it in place. She watched everything I did.

"You made that look easy," she said, raising her gaze to mine with a smile on her lips.

"I've done it a few times," I said, my gaze involuntarily lingering on her red bow-shaped lips.

Both of us seemed to hold our breaths.

I was drawn to her like a bee to honey. There was nothing I could do about that.

As I ducked my head toward hers, her eyes drifted closed.

That was it. I was lost.

I pressed my lips to hers and my whole world righted itself.

I had found my true north.

The kiss was chaste and innocent. The kind of kiss that could change a man's life forever.

"Skye Cessna 123K, Houston Ground, taxi to Runway 45."

The air traffic controller's voice, coming from far away through the headset I wasn't wearing.

I straightened.

"We're being summoned," I said.

Opening her eyes, she nodded. She was not making this easy. I was drawn to her like a sailor drawn to a siren across the deadly rocks.

Saved by the air traffic controller.

I could have sat here and kissed her for the rest of the day. I didn't even care if the airplane moved at all.

But we couldn't just sit here. We had to get in the air.

"We're on our way," I said, smiling over at her.

I had the very distinct feeling that being on our way was rife with several layers of meaning.

Chapter Nine

Anastasia

It was a lovely day for a flight. The sky was clear with just a few white wispy clouds splashed across the sky here and there.

Christopher's takeoff was smooth and he soon took us to ten thousand feet.

I knew that we steadied out at ten thousand feet because he told me. He told me it was his favorite flying altitude because the earth still looked like it was supposed to.

Staring out the window, I could see what he meant. I could see rivers meandering along, roads following along for the most part. Houses. Fields. Any higher and we wouldn't be able to see much of anything. Maybe some colors.

I could still feel his lips against mine. Such a simple, innocent kiss, but it had my whole system in an upheaval.

Looking out the window, I pressed the back of my hand against my lips and replayed that simple kiss over and over.

I was getting in over my head. I could feel it in my bones.

Austin had warned me against Frederick. He hadn't said anything about Christopher, but he didn't know about Christopher. He didn't know and he wasn't here for me to talk to him about Christopher.

I was on my own.

I straightened in my chair and steeled myself.

It wasn't a big deal. I was here to spend an afternoon with Christopher and his family. That was all. It was simple, really.

Just because we were flying halfway across the country together didn't mean anything serious.

To Christopher we could have just as easily been driving.

He was a pilot through and through.

I could tell by the ease with which he handled the airplane controls.

The easy way he spoke to the air traffic controllers.

I was calmer now. Calm, but nervous at the same time.

I'd convinced myself that this trip didn't mean anything. It was a much bigger deal to me than it was to him.

So I would just enjoy myself. I had to admit that I had enjoyed the flight. Sitting up front, watching the world flow by below had been a new experience for me. It was different sitting up front.

Not only had I watched the world below, but I had watched the computer monitors and watched as Christopher made adjustments here and there on the hundreds of knobs and levers.

I knew absolutely nothing about what he was doing.

Maybe I should have studied aviation, at least enough to have a general idea of what Christopher was doing.

If he was like most pilots, his world revolved around flying and airplanes. In order to connect with him, I would need to at least know the basics of his language.

When he brought the airplane down to the runway in a smooth as silk landing, I was officially impressed.

"We're here," he said, smiling at me.

I smiled back. I couldn't help it. I had stared out the window for most of the flight. I hadn't wanted him to see the effect his kiss had on me. The way my cheeks heated and my pulse raced.

We did not however, land at the Denver airport. Instead we landed on a small runway which by no means would I call an airport.

"I'm just guessing," I said. "But I don't think this is the Denver airport."

He grinned. "You are correct. This is Whiskey Springs."

"Whiskey Springs?" This was even more unexpected. We'd just landed on a strip out in the middle of a forest.

"Will your sister pick us up?" I asked as we taxied down the runway.

"Nah. Their old pickup truck is parked in the lot."

I imagined what his old pickup truck must look like. Probably a brand new Chevrolet or maybe a Dodge. My dad kept a truck around to haul things around in. He claimed a man needed access to a truck.

After Christopher completed the post flight checklist, we climbed out of the plane into dry, cool air. So much different from the humid air of Houston.

"The air feels different," I said.

"You've been out west?" he asked as we walked across the tarmac. It smelled the same as the airport in Houston. Like jet fuel. But instead of being loud, it was quiet. With nothing more than wind rustling in the leaves of trees and birds singing.

"No," I said. "I haven't done a lot of traveling."

"Oh," he said. "It's beautiful out here."

"Did you grow up here?" I asked, waiting while he secured the plane.

"Hardly. I'm from Houston. My sister's husband is a successful stock trader and they wanted to move out here."

"Nice."

We turned and then I saw what he had called his old pickup truck.

He had not been exaggerating.

It was an old green pickup truck from the last century. Maybe even the middle of the last century.

I slowed. "That's your truck?"

"My brother-in-law's truck. It's great for hauling firewood."

"Wow."

"Come on," he said. "It's perfectly safe."

After he opened up the passenger door, he put his hands on my waist, lifted me up like it was nothing, and set me on the seat.

While he went around to the driver's side, I buckled up. The truck only had a waist belt. No shoulder harness.

"Are you sure this is safe?" I asked, running a hand over the waist belt.

"We don't have far to go," he said.

"Okay," I said, taking a deep breath. How bad could it be?

I'd just about reached my threshold for surprises, but I had a feeling we were just getting started.

Chapter Ten

CHRISTOPHER

We pulled up in front of my sister's cabin and I parked the old pickup truck off to one side in a dirt parking area beneath some fir trees.

I couldn't help but see the cabin through Anastasia's eyes.

I didn't know where specifically she had grown up—other than it was a small town called Maple Creek—but her grandparents had lived a mansion in the middle of downtown Houston. It was so big and grand and historical that it was now preserved as a historical wedding and special occasion venue.

I'd always liked Charlotte's cabin, but in comparison to the Sterling House, it was small and almost quaint. It didn't matter that it had four bedrooms and a wrap-around deck and was located in one of the most beautiful places in the country.

Anastasia took in everything as we walked toward the door. The little layer of lavender crocuses. The tall yellow sunflowers reaching for the warm sunshine and the mint agastache with blue-green foliage that smelled like licorice and attracted hummingbirds like crazy.

Smoke swirled out of the fireplace into the otherwise clear sky.

The tall Rocky Mountains rose behind the cabin providing a breathtaking background.

"It's beautiful here," she said.

"Yeah? You like it?"

"It's like something out of a painting."

"It is, isn't it?" I asked, proudly. "They like it. I think they go hiking just about every day."

"It would be a really nice place to work," she said.

It wasn't even my house and yet it pleased me that she thought so.

As we reached the front door, it opened and a little girl rushed out, launching herself into Christopher's arms.

Laughing, he picked her up.

"It's so good to see you, Lil," he said, twirling her around in a circle.

"I missed you," she said with a little girl lisp.

"I missed you, too. I want you to meet my friend. Anastasia."

The little girl, cute as a bug's ear, turned in his arms and looked at me. She was wearing a cute little dress and white sneakers and her dark brown hair was pulled back in a bouncy ponytail.

"Hi Anast... Ana."

"Hi Lily. It's nice to meet you."

"Does Mamma know you brought a girlfriend?" Lily whispered loudly in Christopher's ear.

"She does," he said. "She said it was okay."

"Okay," Lily said, scrambling down and taking one of Christopher's hands and one of mine.

I was instantly charmed.

I could see now how Lily had captured Christopher's heart. I'd just met her and already I liked her.

"I'm in the kitchen," Charlotte called out as we stepped through the front door.

"Christopher brought a girlfriend," Lily told her as she led us into the kitchen.

"Good," she said, over her shoulder. "Take them outside to the back deck."

Then she turned to us, wiped her hands on her apron.

"Hi Anastasia," she said. "It's nice to meet you."

"It's very kind of you to have me."

"Wouldn't miss it," she said. "You're the first girl Christopher has ever brought home."

"Char," I said, but it was too late. Between my sister and my niece, I didn't stand a chance.

Maybe this hadn't been such a good idea after all.

"Let's go out back," I said. "and sit on the deck."

Anastasia smiled as we went through the back door onto my sister's deck with the spectacular view.

Chapter Eleven

ANASTASIA

The cabin—a house actually with log walls—was charming. For a log cabin, it was rather large with a wraparound deck. The back deck, however, was as big as another room.

There was a large picnic table and several chairs. It looked like the family spent a lot of time out here.

I could most definitely see why.

The view of the rugged mountain peaks was nothing less than spectacular.

I'd grown up in a small town with a forest in my backyard, but it was nothing compared to this.

The tall mountains were capped with snow, whether it was snow from last winter or if it had already snowed this season, I couldn't say.

The air was so crisp and clean, it nearly hurt to breath it in. It smelled like a spruce and fir tree forest after a rain. Which it was.

We followed Lily over to the picnic table and sat down across from her.

"Do you want to play a game?" she asked, bouncing in her seat.

"Sure," Christopher said, looking at me with a little shrug. "What do you have?"

"It's a card game."

She pulled a stack of oversized cards out of a wooden box and began to distribute them. The cards had pictures of cute, colorful cats on them.

"What's this game?" I asked.

"Old Maid," Lily said. "Do you know how to play?"

"I think I do," I said, glancing at Christopher. "But it's been a long time."

It took her a while to get all the cards dealt, but she seemed quite focused on the task.

"What does the old maid look like?" Christopher asked.

"I can't show you," Lily said. "But you'll know if you get her."

We all picked up our cards and began sorting them.

Charlotte brought out a tray with a pitcher of lemonade and some colorful plastic glasses.

"She's already roped you into her currently favorite game," she said, pouring lemonade into plastic glasses.

"Nice glasses," Christopher said.

"Hard to break," Charlotte said with a little shrug.

"Where is Stanley?" Christopher asked as he pulled a card from his niece's hand.

"Had a meeting in New York," she said.

"New York? Guess he won't be home for dinner."

"He'll be home Tuesday," she said, sliding onto the bench next to her daughter. "Do you have children?" she asked me.

"Me? No." I glanced at Christopher, but he was focused on sorting his cards.

"Changes everything," she said, straightening her daughter's ponytail. "Mostly in a good way."

"Rather limits the travel." Christopher commented.

"I don't mind that. Gives me an excuse to stay home."

"Char paints," Christopher said.

"It's just a hobby," she said. "But I do enjoy it."

"That's very important," I said, tugging a card from Lily's hand. "Wait. I wanted that one."

Lily giggled and turned her cards back so I could take one from the left.

"You have to watch this one," Charlotte said. "She won't cheat, but she'll play her advantages."

"She looks like she has lots of advantages. I think you're going to have your hands full," I said, thinking of my own little sister who had an equal amount of liveliness and cuteness.

"Don't I know it," Charlotte said, rubbing a hand over her stomach. "I have a feeling this one might be a boy, but as long as it's healthy."

"My brother just got married yesterday," I said.

"You'll be an aunt before you know it," Christopher said.

"You're the old maid," Lily said, giggling.

Christopher held up the card with an image of an older cat wearing glasses and holding a cane.

"So that's what an old maid looks like," I said.

"You'll never be an old maid," Lily said. "You're too pretty."

"Thank you. I hope not."

"She won't be," Christopher said, matter-of-factly, shuffling his cards before sliding them over to Lily.

He said it with such conviction that I looked at him, but he was refilling our glasses with lemonade.

"What are you working on now?" Christopher asked his sister. "Do we get to see any of your paintings?"

"Sure," Charlotte said. "Dinner will be ready before long." She turned to Lily. "Go wash up, Lily. Get ready for dinner."

"Okay," Lily said, but before she left, she ran around and gave Christopher another hug.

Then Lily was gone into the house like a flash.

"Well," Charlotte said. "Come on in when you're ready. I'll go check on dinner."

Then she went inside, too, leaving us outside.

I was suddenly acutely aware of being alone again with Christopher. We'd just flown halfway across the country together and being the only two people in an airplane together didn't get much more alone.

But here we were sitting outside his sister's house in a place I'd never heard of. Whiskey Springs, Colorado.

Maybe it was the way he looked at me that made me so aware of him.

Or maybe it was the memory of that kiss. I'd been kissed far more passionately, but I'd never been kissed with what felt like such gentle affection. I'd never been so affected by a simple kiss.

It felt so... caring.

Christopher wasn't like other guys.

He loved his niece and his sister and he was sharing that with me.

"Are you okay?" he asked, taking my hand.

"Yes," I said, swallowing hard.

He was moving fast. It was hard for me to believe that we had only met yesterday. I felt like I had known him forever.

I didn't know what I was going to do about him.

I'd told myself this was just a normal day shared with a nice guy I had just met.

But it felt like something else. Something more.

We sat there, the soft mountain breeze tousling my hair. He kept his gaze on mine, his sparkling blue eyes grabbed hold of mine and didn't let go. It was almost like he could see deep into my soul.

I was falling and falling fast.

Christopher Taylor was like no one I had ever met before.

Chapter Twelve

CHRISTOPHER

Spending the day at my sister's house was something I'd done a hundred times, but today it was different. It was rather funny. I hadn't even realized what I had been missing until today.

Today I had Anastasia with me.

I wanted her here with me and I was going to want her with me from here on out.

My sister made her famous vegetarian lasagna and the scent of garlic bread filled the house.

I sat next to Anastasia and we listened to Lily chatter about nothing in particular while we ate.

"You'll want to fly out before it gets dark," Charlotte said.

"Probably."

"Anastasia," Charlotte said, turning to her. "It was lovely to meet you and I hope you come back soon."

My gaze flicked to Christopher. He was helping Lily pick up plates. Mostly he was picking up plates while Lily trailed along behind him.

"I will," I said, not knowing what else to say.

"I think my sister is running us off," Christopher said.

"It's the job of an older sister to watch out for her younger brother. You know the Whiskey Springs airport is best navigated during daylight."

"You're right," I pulled Anastasia to her feet. "She's right," I told her.

"I really appreciate your kindness," Anastasia said, then looked at Lily. "Thanks for the game of Old Maid."

Lily rushed forward, throwing her arms around Anastasia.

Anastasia knelt down, putting her arms around Lily, hugging her back.

"After you and Christopher get married," Lily said, "we can play Old Maid every day."

Other than a quick widening of the eyes, Anastasia didn't miss a beat.

"Yes," she said. "Yes. We can. And I bet you almost always win."

Lily grinned, then turned and waved. "Bye Uncle Chris."

"Bye Lily. Hey. Where is my hug?"

Lily laughed and gave me a hug. I grabbed her up and swung her around, making her giggle.

Then I gave her a kiss on the cheek and set her on her feet.

"Now go," I said. "And stay out of trouble."

Laughing, she ran up the stairs toward her room.

"It must be good to be an uncle." Charlotte sighed.

"And it's good to be a mother." I hugged my sister. "We'll go now, but we'll be back."

Then Charlotte pulled Anastasia into a hug. "Come back," she said. "You're always welcome. Even without my brother."

Anastasia laughed. "You're very kind."

I took Anastasia's hand and together we went back out to the old truck.

I opened the door and lifted Anastasia into the passenger's seat.

Once I was settled into the driver's seat, I backed out of the parking space.

"Lily and Char really took to you," I said.

"They're very kind and Lily is so sweet. She's going to give her mother trouble when she's a teenager."

"I think she already does give her mother trouble," I said, driving through Main Street. "I'm gonna stop up here and get some coffee. Want some?"

"Sure."

I parked in front of the coffee shop and we went inside together.

It was early evening, still daylight, and the coffee shop was packed.

We stood in line and waited to order our coffee.

"Do you know anyone here?" Anastasia asked.

"Just my sister and her family. That's it."

She nodded and gazed around.

"This reminds me of Maple Creek where I grew up."

"That's right," I said. "Maple Creek. You don't seem like a small town girl."

"What does a small town girl seem like?" she asked with a playful little smile.

"I don't know." I looked around, then leaned close to her and whispered. "You aren't wearing jeans and a flannel shirt."

"I have jeans and flannel shirts," she said. "Just not this weekend."

"I didn't say I had a problem with jeans and flannel," I said. "It just seems like something a small town girl would wear."

"You're right, actually."

We ordered our coffee and stood aside waiting for the barista.

While we waited, I noticed that several of the guys in the coffee shop were looking in her direction.

She definitely stood out—in a good way. Besides being someone they didn't recognize, she didn't look like she was from here.

Anastasia didn't even seem to notice.

She watched the barista making our coffee.

"Christopher and company," the barista said.

"Everyone's a comedian," I said to her before I went up to the counter to pick up our coffees.

My cup had *Christopher* on it, but her cup had *Mrs. Christopher* scrawled on it.

"What is it with people?" I asked, leading her back outside to the street. "Is it because we were at a wedding yesterday? Do we look like we came from a wedding?"

"I think it's a small town thing," she said, setting her coffee inside the truck, then turning around and putting her hands on my shoulders for me to lift her up.

Grinning, I obliged. I liked it that, first of all, she didn't mind, and second of all, that she was coming to expect it.

I liked that very much.

It meant so many different things and I liked every single one of them.

Chapter Thirteen

Anastasia

The flight back to Houston was uneventful. According to Austin, an uneventful flight was the best kind.

By the time we landed at the Houston airport, the stars were shining brightly and the full moon glowed in the sky.

As we taxied down the runway, Christopher turned to me.

"Can I see you again?" he asked.

I almost said *yes*. That was my gut reaction. But then I thought about how I was supposed to be back in Maple Creek, tonight actually. Looked like it was going to be tomorrow though before I got back home.

"I have to work tomorrow," I said.

"So do I."

"I have to be at my desk in Maple Creek for a Zoom meeting."

"And I have to fly someone up to Dallas, wait for them to go to a meeting, and fly back."

"You win," I said.

Christopher laughed. "I'm just sayin'. We both have things to do. I still want to see you."

I looked at him sideways, then looked back out at the terminal. This was his life. Flying across the country. My life was sitting at my computer.

"What will it take?" he asked as he parked the airplane.

"What do you mean?"

"If I lasso the moon and hand it to you, can I see you again?"

"Okay, Jimmy Stewart."

"Does that mean yes?"

He pulled out his iPad and began going through the post flight checklist.

"Yes," I said. "Although I honestly don't see how we can possibly make it work."

"You do know that there is an airport in Maple Creek, right?"

"I'm familiar with it."

"That means anything is possible," he said. "As long as there is an airport."

"You have an interesting perspective on things."

"What can I say? I'm a pilot."

"Truer words were never spoken."

"Are you staying at the Sterling House tonight?"

"Yeah. It's too late to drive to Maple Creek."

"Come on. I'll give you a ride."

"You don't have to do that." I opened up my phone app and scrolled through looking for an Uber.

He put a hand over mine.

"I might be from the city," he said. "but I know that a gentleman always sees the girl home after a date."

A date. I hadn't realized we were on a date.

But now that I thought about it, it had definitely been a date.

He had slipped that right by me under the guise of meeting his family and being swept away by the charm of his niece.

"It's really not necessary," I said.

He looked at me sideways.

"How can I kiss you goodnight if I don't drive you home?"

"Okay," I said, relenting. "You can drive me home."

On the entire drive back to Sterling House, with him deftly navigating traffic in his rental car, I found that there was only one thing I could think about.

Kissing Christopher.

He had me under some kind of spell.

Chapter Fourteen

CHRISTOPHER

Traffic was light at almost eleven o'clock at night on the Houston freeways.

The moon was big and bright. Austin and Ava had picked a perfect weekend for a wedding. Beautiful autumn weather. They weren't here to enjoy it though. Paris, I think they had said.

My ploy to get Anastasia to think about kissing me goodnight backfired.

I didn't know whether or not she was thinking about it, but I certainly was.

We rode in silence, each lost in our own thoughts.

When we pulled up to the Sterling House, the valet and guard were there. Once again, I was instructed where to park.

The valet opened Anastasia's door before I could get around there.

After thanking them, I took her hand and led her toward the door.

"Is your family still here?" I asked.

"I think my grandmother is still here," she said. "It's hard for her to leave. Part of the agreement is that she can visit whenever she wants to and can stay as often as she likes. They let her keep her bedroom."

"I can't imagine how hard it must be for her to let it go. Someone said she's moving in with your family."

"She already has. But she misses the city. Actually I think she misses the life she had here with my grandfather."

I loosely linked a hand with hers. We had reached the front door, standing outside, neither bothering to open the door.

The light breeze was cool and inviting.

"What made her decide to leave?"

"Loneliness. Without Grandpa she just stayed inside and didn't do the things they had done together. They used to visit museums and opera and baseball games. They did everything. But without him, she didn't do those things anymore. So she moved in with us to be with her family."

"I hate that," he said. "But I'm glad she has you all to live with."

"What about your parents?"

"They died when Char and I were in college. It's just us now. It's just been us for a long time. Even with her being married, her husband travels a lot. But she has Lily, so it's better."

"I'm so sorry. I noticed she seemed a little sad."

"She's been that way ever since the accident. It's like a cloud that hangs over her. As long as she has Lily, though, she's okay."

"I can't imagine how hard that must have been."

I wanted to change the subject before she asked how I was doing with the loss of my parents. She, however, beat me to it.

"Have you ever been married?"

"I've never had the inclination," I said.

"You don't want to be married?"

"I do want to be married. But I want to marry the right person."

I took her hand and kissed her palm.

"What about you?" I asked.

"I've never been so inclined either." His kiss was distracting me. "But Lily seems to have other ideas. She seems to think you'll be getting married soon."

"She's five."

"She seems quite convinced."

"I don't know if you noticed or not, but you're the one she seems to think I should be marrying."

"She doesn't know me." She glanced over my shoulder at the valet and guard. They weren't paying us any attention. I had already checked.

"She knows everything she needs to know."

"That I didn't lose at Old Maid?"

"Yes," I said. "That is definitely it. That's how she knows that you and I will be getting married."

She raised an eyebrow at me.

"Like you said," she told me. "everyone is a comedian."

"I'm not trying to be funny."

She was standing with her back to the doorway. I moved to

stand in front of her, blocking her from the view of the two men standing guard.

"I should let you get inside," I said. "It's late."

"Okay." But she didn't move.

I put one hand on the door behind her head and lightly lifted her chin with the other.

"But we have some business first."

"I think you mentioned something," she said, licking her lips.

"I seem to recall it also."

I slowly lowered my face to hers until her eyes closed and our breath mingled.

She was so sweet. So innocent. Maybe I didn't have the right to kiss her like I wanted to.

I pressed my lips lightly against hers.

This would have to do for now.

But her lips were hungry. I felt her wanting more.

And I couldn't resist her. I deepened the kiss. My tongue lightly tracing the outline of her bow shaped lips before plunging deep to touch the roof of her mouth.

She sighed and leaned against me.

We kissed until I heard the men talking behind us.

As much as wanted to kiss her, I wanted to keep her reputation intact even more.

"I have to let you go inside now, Little one," I said.

She nodded and barely opened her eyes. "I know."

I pulled a card, one of my Skye Travels cards out of my pocket and pressed it into her hand.

"Send me your number," he said. "This is my cell number."

"Okay," she said with a little nod.

"Promise me? Send me your number?"

"Okay," she said, sliding the card into her skirt pocket. "I promise."

I kissed her lightly before opening the door and holding it while she stepped inside.

She looked over her shoulder at me before I closed the door behind her.

She would be safe.

There were guards outside the house.

Now I just had to wait until I could see her again.

She had my number and we would figure out when we could get together again.

Soon.

We would get together again soon.

Chapter Fifteen

ANASTASIA

The Sterling House was quiet with only the steady ticking of the grandfather clock echoing through the rooms.

I walked through the shadows, making my way quietly up the stairs to my room.

The house smelled like pine. Not the pine scent of the mountains, but the pine scent of a clean house. The Sterling House had always smelled clean. It helped, I supposed, that my grandparents hired people to keep it that way.

Apparently there were still people employed here to keep things cleaned. The house had been cleaned up so fast—literally overnight —after the wedding and reception, it was like it never happened.

Going inside my room, I walked across to the window and looking out, sighed.

I felt like I was walking on air.

I felt changed. Like my life was going to be different now. The way Christopher kissed me was intoxicating.

It was hard to think about much of anything else.

I didn't know what was going to happen next with him, but I felt good about it. Like everything was going to be okay now.

But mostly I had a strong sense that everything was changed.

With Christopher as a boyfriend, my life would be different. Not that he was a boyfriend. Not yet anyway. With kisses like that, though, I couldn't help but imagine him being my boyfriend.

Reaching into my pocket, I wrapped my fingers around Christopher's business card and pulled it out.

Holding it up in the moonlight, I ran a finger across the raised red airplane and read his name.

Christopher Taylor. Pilot.

His cell phone number below his name.

Simple and clean.

Using the light of the moon, I quickly made a new contact for him and added in his number.

I wouldn't text him right now. He was driving. I'd text him later, but I didn't want to lose his number.

As I got ready for bed, I imagined what a life with Christopher would be like.

With my brother being a pilot, I had a good idea of the pilot's lifestyle. They were on call a lot and had to leave at the drop of a hat if someone needed a last minute flight.

Noah Worthington, though, was good to work for and was a reasonable boss. He understood that people had plans and he respected them as much as he could.

As I brushed my teeth, my thoughts went in a thousand directions.

I would have to go shopping. Other than the outfit I was wearing, I didn't really have any dating clothes. I had some nice shirts and blazers for my Zoom calls, but my wardrobe consisted otherwise mostly of jeans and sweatpants.

And, oddly enough, when I wasn't on a Zoom call, I often wore a flannel shirt.

Christopher knew more about small town life than he might want to admit.

Jeans and flannel shirts.

We could take walks along the trails around my house. We could snuggle on the faux fur rug in front of the fireplace and watch movies or just kiss for hours.

He could take me flying. We could visit new places together.

There were so very many things he and I could do together.

I felt like I had turned the page and revealed a brand new chapter in my life. One I hadn't even seen coming.

Chapter Sixteen

CHRISTOPHER

I had to be at the airport early the next morning to fly one of my regulars up to Dallas. He went up once a month for a board meeting, at a bank I think, and he always had me stay to fly him right back.

I was pretty sure it was a family bank and he only went because of that obligation.

He was a history professor, Dr. Henry Woods, at one of the Houston colleges and attending board meetings didn't seem like something he was really interested in.

Like a lot of my passengers, he rode in the copilot's seat.

"You seem to be in a good mood today," Henry said. He spoke with a slight Irish accent.

"I had a good weekend," I said. "I got rooked into going to another pilot's wedding and while I was there, I met a girl."

"Ah," Henry said. "Weddings are a good place to meet girls. I met my wife at a wedding."

"Did you now?" I put on my headset and listened to the control tower chatter.

Like yesterday, it was a good day for a flight. Blue skies with white wispy clouds. The wind socks hung flat against the poles.

I checked my phone. No messages.

"Yeah," Henry said. "It's not true what they say."

"What do they say?" I asked before I sent an acknowledgement to the control tower that we were clear for takeoff.

"Oh. You know. The usual. They say a relationship that starts at a wedding can never last."

"I've never heard that," I said, checking settings.

"I wouldn't worry about it if I were you. It's probably just an old Irish saying."

"Probably," I said. "People say all sorts of things, don't they?"

"Jenny and I have been married two years and two months. I say let them talk. So tell me about this girl."

I waited until I had the airplane in the air. Then I told him what I knew about Anastasia.

"She lives in Maple Creek and her brother is a pilot."

I was quickly realizing I didn't know much at all about her.

"What does she do?"

"She works from home."

"I see," Henry said, letting it drop, since I obviously had no idea what kind of work she did from home. "Well, I'm glad you met someone. You've been needing to get yourself a girlfriend."

I laughed. "Why do you say that?" I asked. "Maybe I already had a girlfriend."

"Maybe you did, but you've got that look in your eyes." He tapped his own temple. "This one is different."

"You're right about that," I said. "Tell me about today's board meeting."

I wanted to change the subject. Things were still too new with Anastasia for me to feel good about talking about her.

"The usual nonsense. My cousins are a very strange bunch. Did you know that they get upset when kids put soap in the water fountain out in the front of the bank? Why would they want to take such innocent fun away from today's kids?"

"Maybe they'd rather see them stealing from stores or breaking into people's accounts."

"Probably so," Henry said. "What is the world coming to?"

I didn't know what the world was coming to, but I did know that my world had been set aright.

I'd found the girl of my dreams. The girl who made my heart race and my throat dry.

I was going to be like Henry. I was going to marry a girl I met at a wedding.

Chapter Seventeen

ANASTASIA

I had a Zoom call at ten o'clock, so I got in a couple hours of work before then. At ten to ten, I changed my shirt and put on a blazer. Smeared on some lip gloss and ran a brush through my hair.

Appearance wasn't everything, but it was toward the top of the list.

Today I would be meeting with an attorney I had worked for on a steady basis.

As a paralegal, I had three attorneys I worked for. Since they all worked for the same firm, they managed to keep my work load balanced.

I was a researcher. I liked finding precedents that could turn a trial around. I was good at it, too. I had computer programs that I used, but I also had stacks of law books on my desk. I could find things in those physical books a lot of times faster than I could find something online.

It was how I had taught myself in college and it worked out in the world, too.

My grandmother's assistant had grabbed up my outfit from yesterday and sent it to the cleaners. Unfortunately, I'd left Christopher's business card in my pocket. So that was gone.

Fortunately, I'd made a contact for him in my phone.

As I waited for the attorney to come online, I opened up a text for Christopher and typed a message.

> Hey. It's Anastasia. Just sending you my number. Hope you're having a good flight.

I'd have to work on it, but it was a good start.

The attorney came online and I quickly stashed my phone, putting all my attention on him.

An hour later, with several pages of notes to keep me busy, I pulled out my cell phone and unlocked it.

I didn't have any messages. But I had, however, somehow in the process of stashing my phone before the call accidentally sent the message to Christopher.

Well. That wasn't supposed to happen.

But, I decided the message wasn't so bad all things considered. Since he was probably flying right now, I would just have to wait.

I got busy, digging into my research.

It was three o'clock before I came up for air. I loved a challenging case and this was most definitely challenging.

I checked my phone again.

My message was still just sitting there. No response. It didn't even say delivered, but a lot of people turned that feature off. It wasn't unusual.

I went downstairs to find something to eat.

While I was making a grilled cheese sandwich, I got a message from Austin.

> **AUSTIN**
>
> Greetings from Paris. How are things back home?

> Things are good here. Are you having a good time?

> **AUSTIN**
>
> So much to see. I highly recommend it.

> I'll keep that in mind. You're not supposed to be sightseeing so much, are you?

> **AUSTIN**
>
> No comment.

Smiling, I turned off the stovetop and took my sandwich with me to the breakfast table. If there was anyone else home, they weren't around. I usually had the house to myself during the day, so that wasn't surprising, especially since Grandma was still in Houston.

I liked having her here. It made the house less lonely knowing she was around. Puttering in the garden. Or baking something. Or just sitting and reading a book in the sunroom.

> **AUSTIN**
>
> What did you think of Christopher?

I stared at the message.

How did Austin know about Christopher? He'd been completely focused on Ava, as he should have been.

Someone must have seen us together and messaged him.

> Seems like a nice guy.

AUSTIN

I don't know him well. He's new at Skye Travels, but I've only heard good things about him.

> Good to know.

AUSTIN

Got to run. Talk soon.

As I ate my grilled cheese sandwich and watched birds flutter around one of Grandma's bird feeders, I wondered what my brother had heard about Christopher and me.

Did he know that we had gone to Colorado yesterday? I didn't think so. He would have said something.

I couldn't figure out how he knew about him at all.

Maybe it didn't matter. It was getting late and I hadn't heard back from Christopher. Maybe he'd come to his senses and realized that me living out here in Maple Creek wasn't going to work. Maybe he was being practical.

I quickly cleaned up the kitchen and headed back upstairs to work a couple more hours before the rest of the family got home.

It was later that evening when I was relaxing in front of the fireplace with a book, still no response from Christopher, that I sent my brother a quick text.

How do you know about Christopher?

He didn't respond right away. Newlyweds.

CHRISTOPHER

I probably shouldn't tell you, but... I
asked him to watch out for you. To
rescue you from Frederick.

It all made sense now.

The way Christopher cut in on Frederick while we were dancing.

Frederick had not been what I had expected him to be. He'd not only stormed off after I'd sided with Christopher, but he wasn't very considerate and even more, he wasn't very interesting.

He kept asking me inane "Would you rather..." Questions. I was okay with one or two here and there, but it seemed like it was the best he could do as far as conversations went. From the little time I'd spent with him, I deemed him much too shallow for my taste.

I was grateful to my brother for arranging to have Christopher rescue me.

I was not happy with Christopher, however, for taking advantage of that situation and leading me to believe that he actually wanted to have a relationship with me.

Another glance at my phone told me that Christopher had not texted me back.

Well. I wasn't going to worry about it.

If he'd just been there as a favor to my brother, then he had gone above and beyond the call of duty.

I was relieving him of any and all obligations.

I forced my attention back on the novel I was reading.

Told myself it didn't matter.

It didn't keep the hurt at bay.

Chapter Eighteen

CHRISTOPHER

My trip to Dallas and back was uneventful. The best kind of flight.

Henry talked on the way back, telling my about his meeting with what he called his crazy cousins, allowing me to sit quietly.

I thought Anastasia would have sent me her phone number by now.

She had promised. She didn't seem like the kind of girl who wouldn't follow through.

Something could have happened to her. That was where my mind went. I couldn't stop it even if I wanted it to. Since my parents' accident, it was an automatic. It had been nearly ten years since their accident, and even with years of therapy, my thoughts still went there automatically.

After making a smooth landing and getting Henry off the plane and in the car that would take him home or wherever he wanted to go, I finished up my post flight checklist and tried not to think about the possibility of Anastasia getting in an accident on her way home to Maple Creek.

After finishing up my paperwork and securing the plane, I gave in and checked my phone app that would tell me if there had been any accidents today.

There hadn't been any.

Feeling relieved and not a little bit foolish, I got into my rental car and drove to my condo.

As I navigated traffic, I considered my options.

One, of course, was that I could wait. Another option was to drive down to Sterling House, but that didn't make a whole lot of sense because I knew she wasn't there.

A third option was to drive up to Maple Creek. That didn't make a whole lot of sense either since it would be hard to find someone even in a small town.

I could ask around, probably find her, but that didn't sit right with me.

If she didn't want to stay in touch with me, then I had to respect that. The ball was in her court and I had to go with my first option of just waiting.

She had my business card. My number.

She would get in touch with me when she was ready. If she was ready.

I didn't have to like it. I'd been thinking all day about kissing her. Looking forward to kissing her again.

I should have gotten her phone number. At least if I'd gotten her number, I could text her. Maybe she was old-fashioned. There were still a few girls out there who waited for the guy to make the first move.

I'd just thought we were past all that. Maybe I had moved too fast. I was of the mindset that when a person found something they wanted, they should seize the opportunity while they could.

My therapist had assured me that was normal for someone who had experienced the trauma that I had gone through. We'd worked on it and I thought I had my automatic responses under control. Still. Something like losing one's parents in a sudden, horrific way changed the way a person saw the world, no matter how much therapy was involved.

I imagined the conversation I would have with my therapist—just like she said I would—and worked it through.

By the time I pulled into my garage and parked, I had resigned myself to not hearing from Anastasia.

She had made her choice and I had to respect it. I didn't like it, but I knew how to deal with it.

Chapter Nineteen

ANASTASIA

Two weeks later

When Austin and Ava came home from their honeymoon, the whole family was ecstatic. It was like they had been gone for months instead of just two weeks.

It was a pleasant Sunday afternoon in November. Pleasant enough for Father to break out the grill in celebration. Most of the country was already in winter, but not here in south Texas. The sun was shining and it was like a pleasant autumn day.

Birds fluttered about Grandma's birdfeeders, vying for the best spots on the feeders.

Everyone was here except for Jonathan. He'd gone back to work and as usual, he was gone for weeks at the time.

I sat next to Grandma while Ava told us stories of things she and

Austin had seen in Paris while Father and Austin grilled steaks and vegetables.

It should have been one of those moments when I was content. Our family was close and it should have been one of those happy Sunday afternoons when everything was right with the world.

It had been two weeks since I had seen Christopher and I still hadn't gotten a response to my text.

And yet I couldn't shake the yearning I felt for him. I missed him. I felt a little lost without him there.

It was silly, of course. If he didn't want to talk to me, then I had to let him go.

It didn't change how I felt.

When I went inside to grab some already prepared ears of corn for Father to put on the grill, Austin followed me inside.

"Hey," he said.

"Hey." I held the bowl of corn close. "Need something else?"

"What's wrong with you?"

"Nothing," I said. "I'm just tired."

He narrowed his eyes and studied me.

"It's not your tired look," he said. "It's something else."

I shook my head, but I knew he knew he was right.

"Ava's looking for you," I said.

"I know. We'll talk later."

"Okay. Sure." We went back outside together.

I didn't want to talk to Austin. He was too good at reading me. I felt foolish for falling so hard and so fast for Christopher.

I didn't want him to know that I was missing a guy I hardly knew.

Still. As I sat back down on one of the outside chairs, I checked my phone.

No messages other than work related ones.

Before Christopher I hadn't been prone to check my phone a hundred times a day.

That had changed overnight.

And yet no matter how often I checked my phone, I still didn't have any messages from Christopher.

I thought about writing him again.

Maybe he hadn't gotten the message. But I didn't do it. I didn't want to seem desperate.

I wasn't desperate. I had simply gotten the wrong impression that was all.

I think it was when Christopher's sister told me that he'd never brought a girl home before. That had made me think that he liked me. I hadn't helped that Lily had been so sweet and had talked about Christopher and me getting married.

I had to remind myself that she was five.

I had gotten carried away. That was all.

For me, bringing a guy home meant something.

After lunch when Ava projected pictures from her phone onto the large screen television, I plastered a smile on my face and pretended that everything was right with my world.

It would be.

I had my family and that was what mattered.

I'd learned a valuable lesson and as much as I hated to admit that my brother was right, he was.

Pilots were not good dating material.

Chapter Twenty

CHRISTOPHER

Monday mornings were meeting days at Skye Travels.

It was something new that Quinn Worthington, Noah's only son, had started doing as he took over more and more of the running of the business.

Noah still did the hiring, of course, but Quinn—not a pilot—was in charge of the administrative parts of the company.

The pilots who weren't out flying were expected to be in the meetings. The meetings were typically short, just giving us any updates about things like scheduling and there was always an announcement when Noah bought a new airplane or when someone new was hired.

Since I was the last one hired, I knew that firsthand.

Like most Mondays there was coffee and fresh orange juice

along with fruit and granola bars. Skye Travels promoted healthy eating. That was Mrs. Worthington's doing. She watched out for her husband, Noah and for the most part he seemed compliant with his wife's wishes.

I listened as Quinn reported a revamping of the Skye Travels logo. Apparently, even though this was the third rendition of the logo, it was a big deal when changes were made.

Frederick was there, but he hadn't had much to say to me since Austin's wedding. So much for my mentoring. I was okay with it. If I had questions, I could ask anyone here. People at Skye Travels helped each other out. The culture promoted helpfulness over competition.

Besides, I would give up my mentorship with Frederick a million times over for the weekend I'd had with Anastasia, even if it hadn't worked out like I'd wanted.

As we listened to Quinn go through a visual presentation of the different renditions over the years of the Skye Travels logo, I caught Austin watching me.

He was studying me with an intensity that was rather disconcerting, although I couldn't get a sense of what was behind his gaze.

I didn't have any way of knowing what Anastasia had told him, but they were siblings, after all.

Something must have been said.

I wouldn't avoid him, but I wouldn't seek him out, either. I preferred to let things slide in a nonconfrontational way.

Apparently, though, Austin had other ideas.

After the meeting, he cornered me in the supply room where I gone to check out a new pencil for my iPad.

"Hey," he said.

"Hey." I steeled myself. I had not done anything for him to be angry about. I had been a perfect gentleman—for the most part—with his sister.

"Just wanted to thank you for watching out for my sister." He glanced over his shoulder. Lowered his voice. "Rescuing her from Frederick."

"I was happy to do it," I said.

"Yeah." He leaned back against the counter while I logged out the pencil. "Just wondering. Are you seeing anyone?"

"What? No."

"Right. I got that impression. Otherwise I wouldn't have asked you to watch out for Anastasia."

With my new Apple pencil in hand, I turned and faced Austin.

"If I was going to be seeing someone, it would be your sister," I said. There. He could do what he wanted with that information, but I didn't want him thinking I had kissed her and just casually left her. "Unfortunately, the feelings weren't mutual."

"What makes you think they weren't mutual?"

His question took me aback a bit. It wasn't what I expected.

"I gave her my card. Asked her to text me her number. She didn't. It's okay. I understand."

Austin took out his phone and opened up his contacts.

"I think I have your number," he said. "Do you mind checking. Make sure I have it right?"

"Okay." I looked over at his phone where he had my name and a number. "Not my number. My number is 54, not 45."

"Christopher," Austin said, giving me a look as he put his phone away. "You might want to check your business cards. Make sure they're right."

"What are you talking—?"

"I'm just saying. Check your information."

I pulled a card out of my wallet. Handed it to him.

"That's my number."

"Interesting," Austin said as he tucked my card away.

I was beginning to think that there was something wrong with Austin. I'd thought he was an alright guy, but I was starting to think he was weird.

"Anastasia helped me out a few times," he said. "It annoyed me at the time, but now I'm grateful. So I'm going to help you out. It's up to you what you do with it."

My phone chimed.

"That's my sister's cell phone number," he said. "Don't make me regret it."

I stared blankly at Austin's back as he left me standing there.

He'd just given me his sister's phone number.

I pulled out the half a dozen business cards I kept in my wallet. They were all the same and they all had my correct phone number on them.

He was acting like I'd given Anastasia the wrong phone number.

I hadn't, but something had happened. Somehow she and I had gotten our wires crossed.

But whatever had happened, I had Anastasia's number.

I felt like the sun had just come out from behind the clouds.

Chapter Twenty-One

ANASTASIA

It was just a normal Wednesday.

Or would have been except that it was one of those days I had to drive in to Houston for meetings.

I'd gotten into the downtown office at nine o'clock and when lunch time rolled around, I walked down to one of the street side cafés. Since I worked from home, I didn't have a lunch group like most of the regular office workers had.

I was okay with that. I took the opportunity to take a short walk. Since I mostly worked alone, I needed the break from people.

The weather was getting cold. It would be Thanksgiving soon, so the cold weather was coming in right on schedule.

I snuggled deeper into my long wool coat and walked past some construction workers, their loud drills drowning out the sounds of traffic.

Picking a café I'd been to many times before, I took a seat at little round table outside and ordered a lemonade.

While I waited, I people watched, a habit my grandmother had instilled in me when I was a little girl. We would sit at cafés, much like this one and she would have me make up stories about the people we watched.

There was one couple, but most of the people sitting at tables, walking past, were business people. Either alone like me or what looked like small groups of coworkers.

I took my time studying the menu and finally ordered some kind of shrimp casserole that sounded interesting.

As I idly watched three businessmen sitting at a table not far from me, deciding that they were accountants, one of the men caught me looking at them and smiled.

I smiled back, but quickly looked away. Although he probably thought it was, it wasn't a flirtatious move. I didn't like being caught watching people. They had a tendency to take it the wrong way.

Pulling out my cell phone, I scrolled through my messages. Nothing interesting, so I checked the news. Nothing interesting there either.

Out of habit, I checked my text messages. Christopher's number had moved down so that I had to scroll down to find it.

It crossed my mind to just delete it, but I wasn't that dramatic.

It would slowly make its way down the list until it was forgotten.

All but forgotten.

Christopher wasn't someone I would ever forget.

He was indelibly etched into my memory.

"Excuse me. Is this seat taken?"

Startled out of my thoughts, I looked up. Blinked.

Glanced around to get my bearings. Then looked again at the man standing in front of me.

"No," I said. "It's not taken."

"Do you mind if I join you?" Christopher asked, putting his hands on the back of the chair and waiting.

"No," I said, gesturing toward the chair. "Have a seat."

"Thank you," he said, sitting down, leaning his elbows on the table, and just looking at me.

His sparkling blue eyes locked onto mine and he looked at me with an amused expression.

"What are you—? How did you—?" I stopped. Shook my head. "What are you doing here?"

"It's a long story."

"I have time," I said.

"Do you want the long version or the short version?"

With cool wind on my face and warm sun on my skin, I sipped my cool lemonade.

"Short version first."

"Your brother gave me your phone number."

He opened a menu and scanned it. "What's good here?"

"I ordered the shrimp casserole," I said, reeling from his quick change of subject. "But... you're here."

He was wearing his pilot's uniform, I realized. Even his pilot's cap that Noah insisted the pilots wear.

He looked like he belonged at an airport, not at a little café in downtown Houston.

"That gets into the long part of the story," he said.

I nodded. "That makes sense, oddly enough."

He grinned.

"Do you still have my business card by chance?"

"No. Someone took my clothes to the cleaners and it was still in my pocket. But I put your number in my phone."

Christopher reached into his wallet and pulled out one of his cards. Slid it toward me.

"Okay," I said, picking up the familiar card.

"Is that the number you have in your phone?"

"I think so," I said, opening up my phone to compare the two. "No."

I looked at him accusingly.

"I didn't do it," he said with a little laugh.

I scrolled down to the text I had sent him and held it up for him to see.

"I texted you," I said.

"And I didn't get it."

I sat back, studied him.

"My brother gave you my number, but you didn't call me. Or text."

"It seemed too impersonal," he said with a little shrug.

When the server stopped by, he ordered his own shrimp casserole.

"I don't understand how you found me," I said.

"That's one of those things I'll tell you after we've known each other for a number of years."

I tried unsuccessfully not to smile.

He was much too charming.

And I was much too happy to see him.

Chapter Twenty-Two

CHRISTOPHER

After lunch, I walked Anastasia back to her office.

"You like downtown Houston?" I asked.

"I do," she said, her skin flushed prettily from the chill in the wind.

"What is it you like?"

"It reminds me of New York."

"Yeah," I said. "It is sort of like New York. Have you spent much time there?"

"I've never been," she said.

It was loud, so we stopped talking as we walked past some construction workers using jackhammers.

"I'll take you to New York," I said as the loud construction sounds faded into the background.

"You don't have to do that."

"I'd like to do it. I've been a few times, but I've never done the touristy things. I'd like to do them with you."

"Okay," she said, absently.

"You don't believe me, do you?" I asked.

"I guess I'm still trying to wrap my head around you being here."

"I'm here," I said. "Here." I pulled my phone from my pocket and sent her a quick message.

Have dinner with me.

"What's that?" she asked, looking at her screen.

"Have dinner with me. Tonight."

"I can't. I have to drive back to Maple Creek after work."

"Tomorrow then."

She looked at me sideways. We had reached her building and stood outside the glass doors. People coming and going around us as though we weren't even there.

"Tomorrow I'll be in Maple Creek."

"They don't have restaurants in Maple Creek?"

She glanced around. Shoved her hair out of her face.

"Nothing like here."

"It's okay. I'll pick you up tomorrow. Just send me your address."

"You'll drive to Maple Creek?"

"I'll figure something out."

She blew out a breath.

"You're rather persistent."

"I have lost time to make up for."

She nodded slowly.

"Okay. I'll text you my address. But I have meetings until four o'clock."

"I'll be there at five."

"Okay," she said, turning to go inside her building. She looked back at me over her shoulder. "I'll see you at five o'clock."

I grinned.

But I had a feeling that if I didn't show up tomorrow, she would no longer trust me.

Fortunately I was good at keeping appointments.

A pilot had to be good at keeping schedules.

Our whole world revolved around schedules and appointments.

I would be there.

Chapter Twenty-Three

ANASTASIA

I played the radio all the way home to Maple Creek and let my mind wander.

I'd had to work hard to stay focused during my last meeting. I'd had to almost physically put Christopher out of my thoughts.

But now, driving home beneath the sliver of moonlight and the sprinkling of stars, I was free to think about Christopher as much as I wanted.

I couldn't figure out how he had found me in downtown Houston. That had taken some skill. I could understood if he'd found me in Maple Creek. In Maple Creek, I would have been easy to find. All he had to do was to ask around. Most everyone knew my family.

I also understood Austin giving him my phone number.

I'd finally relented and told Austin about him. Not everything.

Not the kisses. Those were mine. But I'd told him about visiting his sister in Colorado and I'd told him about not getting a text response.

Since I had been instrumental in helping Austin and Ava get back together, he probably thought he owed me a favor.

I hadn't asked, but I hadn't had to. My brother knew me, sometimes better than I knew myself.

However it had come about, I had a date with Christopher tomorrow.

He'd be showing up at my house at five o'clock.

I'd already texted him my address. I didn't want any crossed wires this time. And he had sent me a quick "see you tomorrow" text.

As I turned off the interstate onto the rural highway, I realized I needed something to wear. What did someone wear on a date in Maple Creek? And not just a date in Maple Creek, but a date with a pilot from Houston?

That changed the whole thing.

I'd ask Ava. Ava would know.

In fact, when I went through the back door, Ava was conveniently sitting at the kitchen table, doing something on her computer. I didn't know what their long-term plans were, if they had any yet, but they had been staying here since they'd gotten back from Paris.

"Hi," I said, taking off my coat and hanging it up in the coat closet.

"Hey," she said, closing her computer. "How was work in the big city?

"Work was... uneventful," I said, borrowing pilot's terminology.

Ava smiled. "The best kind."

"Exactly." I slid into the chair next to hers. "The day, however, was anything but."

"In a good way... or...?"

"A good way," I said, taking a deep breath and letting it out slowly.

"Do you remember Christopher?"

"Of course I do," she said. "He was your designated guardian at our wedding."

"You knew about that?" I asked.

"I was in on it," she admitted.

"Well." I sat back. "He's picking me up here tomorrow. For a date."

"You're kidding." She grinned.

"Nope. Not kidding."

"Wow. That is so exciting."

"Maybe," I said, trying to seem nonchalant. "I need your help."

"Anything," she said.

"What does a girl wear on a date in Maple Creek?"

Ava looked at me a moment.

"No," she said.

"No?"

"No. You're not going on a date in Maple Creek."

"I don't understand."

Ava leaned forward, her hands half hidden in the long sleeves of her comfortable sweatshirt.

"You're going on a date with a pilot. They don't do things like the rest of us."

I shook my head.

"You could be going anywhere."

"You think he's going to take me flying somewhere."

"The odds are good. Very good." She shoved a plate of cookies toward me. "Want a cookie? Grandma made them today."

"No. Maybe." I picked up one of the lemon cookies on the plate. Took a bite.

"Good, huh?"

"Very. So what do I do? How do I dress for a date that could be anywhere?"

"You do just that," she said. "You dress for a date that can be anywhere. Don't worry. I'll help you."

If I trusted anyone to help me, I trusted Ava. I'd known her for years and Ava knew things. It was still something of a mystery what she saw in Austin, but she was one of the smartest people I knew.

This date was going to work out just fine.

Chapter Twenty-Four

CHRISTOPHER

Even though I didn't know what Anastasia and I were going to do. Maybe just hang out at her house and watch a movie after grabbing something at one of the local Maple Creek restaurants. I went with a tux. I figured a guy could never go wrong with a tux.

If she came out in jeans and a flannel shirt, I would just take off my jacket and be good to go.

If I'd owned a flannel shirt, I would have brought it with me just in case, but I didn't. Maybe we could go shopping and she could pick one out for me to wear.

I was a little nervous as I neared her house. Not so much about her, but because she lived with her family.

Austin included.

Austin, as her big brother, made me a little nervous.

Turns out, Maple Creek had at least one Uber and I was able to secure it.

The driver assured me that he would come back if I needed him to.

"Actually," I said, before stepping out of the open door. "If you would just hang out here for a bit?"

"The meter's running, just so you know."

"That's okay. If my plans change, I'll let you know."

"I'll be waiting right here until I hear from you."

"Thanks," I said and headed up the sidewalk to the front door.

Ava opened the door. Her new wedding ring sparkling on her finger.

The house was big. That was my first impression. Not as big as the Sterling House, though, and certainly not as pristine. This was a home. Inviting.

It smelled like cinnamon and vanilla. Candles maybe.

And there were fresh daffodils in a vase on a little table, adding their sweet scent to the mix.

The foyer, like the Sterling House, had a tall grandfather clock standing next to wide stairs leading up to the second floor.

"Hi," Ava said, stepping back to let me in. "Good to see you again Christopher."

"Good to see you, too, Mrs. Devereaux."

She grinned. "Can I take your coat?"

"Sure." I shrugged out of my coat and after handing it to her, she hung it in a coat closet.

"How's married life?"

"Married life is great," she said. "You should give it a try."

"Maybe I will."

As we walked through the foyer, a movement at the top of the stairs caught my attention. Stopping, I looked up and all coherent thought left my head.

Anastasia stood at the top of the stairs.

My instinct to wear a tux had been right. She was wearing a red floor length dress that hugged her lithe body. It had a high neckline, but it was ever so sexy.

She wore white gloves that covered her arms up to her elbows.

She smiled and my heart did summersaults.

We stood there, our eyes locked for what must have been at least a minute, but could have been ten minutes. It was one of those moments when time hovered without boundaries.

I glanced back to say something to Ava, but she was already gone.

Anastasia was most definitely not dressed for hanging out in front of the fireplace or even having dinner in Maple Creek. I couldn't imagine that there was a place in Maple Creek where we could go that we wouldn't be out of place, dressed the way we were.

I walked to the bottom of the stairs to wait for her.

She carefully made her way down the stairs until she stood on the bottom step, face to face with me.

"Hi," I said.

"Hi."

"You look stunningly beautiful."

"You look nice yourself."

I took her hands and assisted her in taking the last step to the floor.

"Do you like opera?" I asked.

"Opera," she said. "Sure."

I tucked her hand in the crook of my arm and together we went out to the Uber.

Chapter Twenty-Five

Ava had been right. Christopher had not picked me up with plans for dinner in Maple Creek. Not wearing a black tux.

There was no place in Maple Creek where a tux would be appropriate attire.

I wasn't the least bit surprised when the Uber he had waiting took us straight to the airport.

The airplane, a little Cessna, sat waiting for us at the Maple Creek Airport.

As he took the airplane up, off the ground in a smooth takeoff, I wondered just how easy it would be to get used to this lifestyle.

With both of my brothers being pilots, I had no doubt that I had at least a touch of flying in my blood. I'd be more surprised if I didn't.

The sun was to our right as we made the short flight down to the Houston airport where he had another car waiting, this one with a chauffeur.

He held my hand in the back seat of the car as the driver headed toward downtown. There was enough traffic to slow us down to a crawl as we entered the theatre district.

I didn't ask where he was taking me. I didn't want to break the spell that seemed to surround us.

He'd asked me about the opera, and if we were going to the opera, then I was okay with it.

I didn't really care where we went. I was content to just ride around with him, holding his hand.

The driver, however, soon pulled up in front of the Houston Grand Opera and we got out of the car.

Christopher pulled two tickets out of his pocket and we went right in, walking past the line at the box office without stopping. This was not a seat of the pants date for him. I was impressed by the level of detail he had put into everything.

I was even more impressed when we sat in a box near the stage.

There were four other people already seated in the box, but we sat near the front.

"Do you always sit in box seats?" I asked, leaning close to Christopher.

"I've never been here," he said.

"Oh." I looked at him sideways and wondered how that could be. He seemed to be right at home and to know just where he was going.

"I had some help," he said.

"I'm impressed," I said.

The orchestra was warming up, playing discordant music that was oddly quite good.

"Thank you," I said.

"For what?"

"For this," I said. "For everything."

"You're welcome." He leaned over and kissed me on the cheek, sending my thoughts down another route. A route that involved lots of kisses.

A route that had me thinking it was too bad there were other people in our box.

I straightened and pulled myself together. Sitting at the opera was not a good place to be thinking about making out with my new boyfriend.

And even though he wasn't a boyfriend exactly, at least not yet, if I were to imagine the perfect boyfriend, that perfect boyfriend would be Christopher Taylor.

Chapter Twenty-Six

CHRISTOPHER

It was my first opera. Not being a flashy kind of guy, when I did go out, I tended to go to movies or a quiet bar with a pool table. I'd been to the rodeo a couple of times and several Astros games. It didn't take anything fancy to entertain me.

I was a man of uncomplicated needs.

My instinct had told me that a girl whose grandmother owned the Sterling House, however, would need more than a movie to entertain her.

I'd had some help. Austin, a product of the same world Anastasia had grown up in had been quite helpful. He'd gotten Ava involved and between the three of us, we'd planned a perfect evening.

I hadn't been sure how it would come off, though. A lot

depended on whether Ava convinced Anastasia to wear an evening gown. Apparently Ava had pulled it off.

I'd been prepared either way.

Not having been to an opera before, I found it surprisingly pleasant.

Although I couldn't understand the words, the emotion in the opera singers' voices was raw and went straight to my heart.

Everything, the costumes, the scenes, was extravagantly done. And yet I spent more time watching Anastasia than I did the stage.

Her facial expressions mirrored the emotions in the music, in the voices.

Toward the end, when Anastasia's eyes teared up, I reached over and took her hand.

She glanced at me as though she had forgotten I was there, then turned her attention back to the performance.

After the opera was over, we made our way back to the car where the driver waited for us.

The driver deftly navigated traffic to get us on the Interstate heading back to the airport.

Anastasia and I sat in the back seat in what felt like startling quiet after the opera.

"Do you know Italian?" I asked.

"No. Do you?"

"Not a bit. You just seemed to understand what they were singing about."

"It was lovely," she said. "And it's easy to feel the emotions in their voices. You don't have to understand the words. Don't you think?"

"I agree completely," I said, although I had felt the emotion through Anastasia's expressions more than anything else. Or maybe it had been a combination of her expressions and the intensity of the music.

Whichever it was, I had to agree that the opera was lovely. I didn't regret bringing her and I had enjoyed the experience myself.

"What other things do you like to do in the city?" I asked.

"I don't know," she said. "My grandparents took us to museums and art exhibits. My grandfather had an affinity for baseball games. My grandmother liked the museums and gardens and things like that. Grandpa went along wherever she wanted to go and she did the same. Going with him to baseball games."

"Sounds like they had a good marriage."

"They loved each other very much," she said, her eyes moist.

And that, I knew was the thing she was looking for in a relationship.

The same thing I was looking for.

I squeezed her hand as we neared the airport.

She looked over and smiled at me in the shadows.

I'd been looking for her my whole life.

I'd go to as many operas and museums as she wanted to. Just as her grandfather had done for her grandmother.

Chapter Twenty-Seven

ANASTASIA

The short flight back to Maple Creek was uneventful. There was a stark contrast between the hurried, crowded Houston Airport with five runways and eleven thousand acres for the dozens of commercial and private airlines that traveled in and out, and the small little deserted, unlit runway at Maple Creek.

All in all, with the taxiing and waiting, it wasn't any quicker to fly to Maple Creek than it was to drive it, but it was definitely different.

"What are you doing Friday evening?" Christopher asked as he went through the post flight checklist.

"Nothing in particular," I said.

"I was thinking I could drive up. Maybe we could hang out. Watch a movie."

"You're going to drive?" I asked.

"I'm thinking about buying a car and thought I'd try it out."

I turned and looked at him with disbelief.

"You don't own a car?"

"Never have. I've always taken Ubers or lately rented a car."

"Wow. I didn't know that someone could live in Texas without a car."

"It baffles a lot of people," he said. "But what do you think? Are you up for a movie?"

"That actually sounds nice," I said. And it did. It would be nice to spend some time with Christopher without having to get dressed up and travel.

So far all our dates had involved one or the other or both.

"Our car's here," he said, when headlights turned off the main road and came toward us.

"Unless it's the police," I said.

"Why would the police be coming out to the airport?"

"I wouldn't know. Not personally. But a lot of my friends used to hang out here after high school dances and such. They often got run off."

"Your friends, huh?"

I grinned. "They told me things."

"I bet they did."

The car turned out to be our ride, nonetheless.

We sat side by side in the back seat as the Uber driver pulled up in our circle drive.

"I'll walk you to the door," Christopher said, getting out and coming around to the other side of the car.

While the driver waited, he walked me to the door.

The light was off, but as we neared, a motion sensor light turned on.

"So much for being discreet," he said.

"I know, right?" I agreed with a hand over my eyes to shade them.

"I'll see you Friday night?" he asked.

"Friday night."

Then, motion porch light and all, he lowered his head to mine and kissed me.

Chapter Twenty-Eight

CHRISTOPHER

When I got to Anastasia's house on Friday, I was in for a surprise.

Instead of being met at the door by Anastasia, I was met by Austin.

I had what was no doubt an instinctual gut reaction that had me immediately on edge.

Austin wasn't Anastasia's father, but he was her brother and that was close enough for me. Too close for comfort.

"Hey," Austin said. "Come on in."

"How's it going?" I asked, pushing aside the knee-jerk reaction to turn around and get back in my car, and instead stepped inside.

"New car?" he asked before closing the door behind me.

"Yeah," I said. "Seemed like a good time to break down and buy one."

Actually buying a car had been far more simple and yet far more complex than I had expected.

It took me ten minutes to pick one out online, but it took two hours to complete the paperwork at the dealership. Probably something to do with it being my first car purchase, but they assured me it always took this long. I didn't find that the least bit comforting and decided that I would run the wheels off this car before I went through that tortuous process again.

"Guess you finally found a reason," Austin said.

"Guess so," I said, looking around for Anastasia.

"She'll be down in a minute," Austin said, going to the coat closet. He pulled out a couple of flannel jackets, tossed one to me. "Might want to wear this."

"Why?"

"It's cold outside." Austin shrugged into one of the flannel jackets.

"You're taking me outside?" I asked, the trepidation returning as I remembered the old saying about two going out and one coming back.

"We're all going," Austin said.

Ava came around the corner, already wearing a wool coat.

"Hey Christopher," she said with a smile.

"Hi Ava." At least Christopher wasn't taking me out to kill me over kissing his sister. "Austin tells me we're going out for a walk."

Ava laughed. "Sounds worse than it is."

As I put on the flannel jacket, I caught sight of Anastasia bouncing down the stairs.

She was dressed adorably cute in jeans and a blue flannel shirt. Her hair was pulled back in a ponytail.

She came right up to me and smiled, but didn't touch me.

"Hi," she said.

"Hi." I would have kissed her if her brother and sister-in-law hadn't been standing right there watching us with curiosity.

"Slight change of plans," she said.

"Okay. I kind of got that impression." I shrugged in my flannel jacket. "Is it a surprise?"

"We're going out to get a Christmas tree."

"Oh. Okay. That's a relief. Going into town then?"

"No, Silly. We're going to the woods to chop one down."

"That's different," I said. Even my sister who lived in a small town, bought her tree at the General Store.

"Come on," she said, sliding a hand into the crook of my elbow. "It'll be fun."

"I have no doubt," I said as all four of us headed out the door.

"New car?" Ava asked.

"Got it yesterday," I said.

"Nice."

"You bought a new car?" Anastasia asked as we walked past. "Just like that?"

"It wasn't a big deal." Although it had turned out to be. "Looks like I have a need for a car now."

Anastasia smiled and looked away.

I wish I knew what she was thinking. I'd love to know what was going on in her head.

It was one of those things about being in a new relationship. Not being sure about what the other person was thinking.

Ten minutes later, after a quick stop by a shed behind the house,

Austin walked along, nonchalantly carrying an axe over his shoulder.

I was just thankful he hadn't answered the door with an axe.

Chapter Twenty-Nine

ANASTASIA

With it being their first Christmas as a married couple, Austin and Ava were intent on finding the perfect Christmas tree for their first Christmas. They wandered through the woods, analyzing tree after tree.

With it being one of our first dates and our first time taking a walk together, Christopher and I hung back, taking our time, just enjoying each other's company.

A couple of squirrels darted across the trail in front of us, racing up one of the maple trees. The trees still had a few brightly colored leaves hanging from their limbs, but most of the leaves were on the ground, tossed about as we walked among them.

"Fall is my favorite time of year," I said.

"What do you like about it?" Christopher asked, taking my hand.

"I know most people think of spring as a time of new beginnings, but I think of fall as new beginnings. New school clothes, new classes. The start of a new season. It's probably silly."

"I don't think it's silly at all," Christopher said. "It's the start of the holidays and the end of brutally hot summer weather."

"Spoken like a true southerner," I said, smiling over at him.

"Only a southerner can truly understand the brutal heat?"

"Exactly."

"Do you think they're going to find a tree?" Christopher asked.

"They'll find something." Although I said it with confidence, I glanced up at the sky. The sun would be going down soon, so they had to find a tree pretty quickly or come back another day.

"We found it," Ava called out from up ahead.

"Guess that answers that," Christopher said. "Think they need our help?"

"I don't know about our help, but I'm sure they need our opinion."

"You're such an optimist. So I guess we should go give them our opinions." Christopher took my hand and we headed toward the sound of the axe. "I have to admit that seeing Austin with an axe has me a little nervous."

I laughed. "Austin is harmless."

"Good to know."

"Timber!" Austin called as we neared the tree he was chopping.

Christopher shoved me behind him, but the tree hit the ground in the opposite direction.

Although we hadn't been in any danger, I felt protected.

Christopher was always protecting me. Starting with the first time we'd met when he'd protected me from Frederick by trying to cut in on the dance floor.

"Come give us a hand," Austin said. "Ava. Don't be pulling on the tree."

"I'm okay," Ava said.

Austin shot her a look and she held up her hands and backed off. "Okay. Okay. Christopher can help you drag the tree."

Going to stand next to Ava, I watched the two guys grab hold of the tree and started dragging it.

"Could have picked a bigger tree," I said with a bit of sarcasm.

"It's for the parlor," Ava said, defending the tree. It was becoming clear that the tall tree had been her choice.

We followed along behind the guys dragging the tree.

"You like Christopher?" Ava asked.

"He's okay," I said, watching as he walked alongside my brother, neither one of them having any trouble dragging the heavy tree.

"Just okay?"

I smiled. "What's not to like?"

"He's a handsome man," she said.

"Stop it." I bumped her elbow. "You're a married woman."

"Doesn't stop a girl from appreciating a handsome man."

"Since you're married to my brother," I said. "I'm going to pretend we didn't have this conversation."

Ava just grinned.

"When did Austin become so protective?" I asked, changing the subject.

"About what?"

"He didn't want you pulling on the tree."

"You know how Austin can be," she said, her skin glowing with the cool air.

"I guess."

It sounded like something she'd tell me about when she was ready. We might live in the same house, but not everything was my business.

"Anyway," Ava said. "Christopher bought a car for you."

"He didn't buy it for me."

"Let me say it another way. He bought it *because* of you."

"I don't think so." But maybe he had. He said he had a reason now. Maybe I was the reason.

It was odd to think that I would be the reason someone would buy a car, especially someone I liked.

Chapter Thirty

CHRISTOPHER

After we got the Christmas tree set up in its stand, Austin ordered pizza.

Sitting at the kitchen table, we played a game of UNO while we waited for the delivery.

"Draw two," Anastasia said, putting down a card. Unfortunately she was playing before me.

The kitchen was cozy and smelled like freshly ground coffee.

I took two cards from the deck and added them to my hand.

"Yellow," Ava said, putting down a Wild Card.

"Sorry," Anastasia said. "I don't have any yellows." Then she proceeded to slap a Draw Four down.

"Thanks," I said. "I needed some more cards."

"Just trying to watch out for you."

"I'd hate to see how you treat your enemies," I said, taking four cards and adding them to my hand.

The next card she played was also a Draw Two.

"I'm beginning to think this is personal," I said.

"I don't know what you mean," Anastasia said, batting her eyelashes prettily.

"You know exactly."

"I can help you out," Austin said, putting down a reversal card.

"Thank you Austin." I looked through my cards. "I don't have any blues." I had to draw three cards before I picked up a blue Reversal Card.

"Can't say I didn't try," Austin said.

"Okay," Anastasia said. "I'm all out of draw cards." She put down a simple number card.

"I feel so fortunate to get to play," I said.

"UNO," Ava said.

I shot Anastasia a look.

She laughed and leaned over to whisper something to me.

"Don't worry. I have a plan."

She put down a card I didn't recognize.

Ava groaned. "Not fair."

"What's that?" I asked.

"It's a Wild Shuffle card."

"I don't know this one."

"We put all our cards together, shuffle them, and deal them," she said.

"This hardly seems fair," I said.

"See. I agree," Ava said. "It's not fair."

"What's not fair about it?" Austin asked. "It's an excellent tactic."

"Just a word of warning," Ava said. "These two." She pointed a finger between Anastasia and Austin. "They might go at each other, but don't ever try to stand between them."

"Don't worry," I said. "I have a sister. But still..."

"It changes when you take a wife," Austin said.

"Good to know."

Twenty minutes later, right after Ava won the game after all, the pizza arrived at the door.

"I didn't know you had such a cutthroat side," I said as Austin and Ava went to the front door to get the pizza.

"UNO is a Devereaux thing," she said. "But didn't you notice? I saved you."

"I see. By giving me a handful of cards."

"We needed them to go after Ava."

"She still won."

"True. But that's not my fault."

"Remind me not to play UNO with you again."

"You'll get the hang of it," Austin said, setting the box of pizza on the table. "Once you realize that the women always win, you'll be okay."

"It's not that bad," Ava said.

"It's that bad," Austin said, passing out plates.

Frankly I didn't care if the women won.

I found it rather sexy that Anastasia had that unexpected playful side to her.

"I hope you don't mind," Ava said. "We're going to turn in early and leave you two to watch the movie."

"We don't mind?" Anastasia asked, turning to me. "Do we?"

"I don't mind. I'm good either way."

I'd been wondering if we would have to share our movie with the newlyweds. I was glad that we didn't, but it would be rude to say so.

It would definitely be rude to say that I'd been looking forward to having Anastasia all to myself.

Chapter Thirty-One

Anastasia

It wasn't my fault Christopher let me pick the movie, but he didn't seem to mind that we watched a romance.

Not only did he not complain, he seemed to enjoy it.

My brothers would have complained.

Not that they wouldn't have liked it, but they seemed to feel obligated to complain when anyone picked a romance movie. Which was usually me.

It seemed necessary to balance out their action movies.

I figured I'd get Christopher started off on the right foot so he'd know what to expect.

At the end of the movie, both of us teared up. I had a lump in my throat so strong that I had to turn away.

As the credits rolled, I swallowed the lump in my throat. Stared at the flames in the hearth and tried to force my mind to go blank.

"That was a good movie," Christopher said.

"You liked it?" Some of the sadness from the movie was replaced with happiness that he liked my kind of movies.

"I did. It's the kind of movie my sister likes, so no, I don't mind. But this one really stabbed deep in my heart."

"The best ones do," I said.

"Seems to be the case."

"What made you buy a car all of a sudden?" I asked, needing to change the subject.

"I had places to go."

"You had a rental car."

He stretched his legs out and stared at the muted advertisement on the television.

"Remember that thing I told you about? The thing that happened with my parents when I was in college?"

"Of course." He had to mean when his parents had been in a car accident.

"Well. What I didn't tell you was that when the accident happened, they'd been driving the car they had just bought for me. A gift for my upcoming graduation. They'd been on their way to bring it to me when the accident happened."

"Oh my God. Christopher. That's awful. I'm so sorry."

"That's the day I swore I would never own a car."

"But you... you just bought a car. The first one?"

"I wanted to be able to drive up to see you without worrying about whether or not I had a rental car."

I put a hand over his.

"You didn't have to do that."

"I'm glad I did." He turned and looked into my eyes. "It feels like I've moved on. Like I finally put that behind me."

I moved closer and curled into him, resting my head on his chest. He wrapped his arms around me.

"You're good for me," he said.

Had I ever been good for anyone before? Not that I could remember. I'd just been another girl.

I sighed against his chest. Christopher was different.

"You're good for me, too."

"I'm thinking we should stick together. What do you think?"

"I think I like that idea."

Chapter Thirty-Two

CHRISTOPHER

Driving home, the music loud, in my new car, I replayed the movie Anastasia had picked out for us to watch.

I got the feeling that she thought I wouldn't want to watch a romantic movie.

Romantic movies were my favorite kind. My sister and I watched them together all the time. And now I had a girl to watch them with.

Besides replaying the movie in my head, I replayed our goodnight kiss. Why were goodnight kisses such good kisses? I wouldn't say that they were the best kind, but they were certainly at the top of the list.

It had to be because they were so bittersweet.

But I would see Anastasia again tomorrow. I was going back to spend the day with her. Ava wanted to decorate the tree and she wanted us all to help her.

I was more than glad to help, especially since it involved spending time with Anastasia. I'd do just about anything to get to spend time with her.

I thought of her as my girl now.

It was probably a sentiment I should share with her. Having a girlfriend had to be a two-way street.

I exited the interstate, turning down Memorial toward my condo. There wasn't a lot of traffic this time of night, making the drive a whole lot easier.

The problem was that I didn't want Anastasia to just be my girl-friend. I wanted more.

It was probably too soon to be thinking about marriage.

According to conventional wisdom we should have a long courtship. Make sure we were right for each other.

I already knew that we were right for each other.

Besides, conventional wisdom was hypocritical. Our society was all about doing everything fast.

We had fast food. Accelerated education. Instant gratification everything. Want to watch a movie? Stream it. Read a book? Download the ebook. Place an order for pretty much anything and get it later that day.

Airplanes, for God's sake, to get us places quickly.

Why, then, I couldn't help but wonder, did we put such restraints on our relationships? I saw no reason why we should wait.

Life was too short.

When I thought about my parents, thought about how little time they'd had together. They had waited to get married. They'd often told the story of how they'd had a five year engagement. It was what their parents expected of them.

So they waited. And then their lives ended unexpectedly just after their twenty-third anniversary. Life was too uncertain. Too fleeting.

I couldn't do that.

I wouldn't do that.

Pulling into the garage, I parked my car.

I was a seize-the-moment kind of guy and I had my reasons. If anyone didn't like it, they could take themselves and their opinions elsewhere.

Nothing said we had to wait.

From where I was sitting, I saw every reason to take advantage of the moment.

Waiting and putting things off was for other people.

I chose not to wait. I chose to cut in line if I had to.

Cutting in line had been the best thing I had ever done.

Cutting in line had gotten me Anastasia.

Epilogue

ANASTASIA

Six Weeks Later

I hadn't been one of those little girls who planned their wedding. Growing up, I honestly hadn't given much thought to the possibility even that I would get married.

It just wasn't something I had thought about.

Having two older brothers didn't help.

My brothers certainly didn't talk about weddings and my younger sister was much too young for that. She was still playing with dolls when I started college.

But... if I had thought about getting married, I would have thought about getting married at Christmastime.

Christmas was my favorite time of the year. It was that time when everyone seemed to be happy and full of joy.

It just made sense that Christmas would be a good time to get married.

If I ever thought about it.

But I didn't.

Except now it was Christmas and I was wearing a traditional ball gown style wedding dress in traditional white.

The Sterling House was decorated in festive reds and silvers. It looked like a fairy tale. Somehow fairy tales had been my theme. A Christmassy fairy tale.

Silver and red. Those were my colors.

My bouquet was the prettiest I had ever seen with little rose buds and little silver foliage. Long silver and red ribbons woven through the flowers and falling along the sides.

A four piece orchestra in the ballroom played romantic Christmas music.

And then there were the festive Christmas trees. Four of them. Four Christmas trees. One in the foyer. One in the parlor and two on either side of the ballroom.

There were a lot of people here. People that Christopher worked with. People that I worked with. People that Grandma knew.

And photographers. I'd seen three of them roaming about. There would be formal pictures later.

So there were a lot of people at my wedding, but not all that many people at my wedding that I knew.

But I was okay with that. I didn't care.

There was only one person here that mattered.

Christopher.

My groom.

We stood at the cake table, admiring the cake that was in the form of a castle with a horse and carriage at the bottom.

"How did they make this?" Christopher asked.

"I don't know. My Grandma knew someone who knew someone through her baking classes."

"She's an amazing woman."

"I agree," I said. "It's like a fairy tale."

"That's our theme."

Glancing up, I saw my grandmother dancing with an older gentleman. I squeezed my eyes, then opened them again. "I think I'm imagining things."

"I don't think so. I know that fellow. He's a widower. A good guy."

"But... I haven't seen my grandmother like this. Not since..."

"It's just a dance," Christopher said, hearing the alarm in my voice. "It's good for her."

I turned to my new husband.

"That's what she told me at Austin's wedding. It's the very thing that led to me meeting you."

"Like I said, she's an amazing woman. Come here."

He pulled me into his arms.

"Be happy for her."

"I am happy for her. I'm just surprised."

"I know." He gently massaged my back. "I don't care what they say, I'm not shoving cake in your face."

"Thank you."

"You're far too beautiful to have cake on you and besides, it's just plain mean."

"How did I get so lucky?" I asked, pulling back and looking up into his blue eyes.

"I'm the lucky one," he said. "I got you."

The music changed.

"I love this song," I said with a little sigh.

"It's one of my favorites," Christopher said.

I nodded. Because Christopher didn't know how to dance, we had skipped the traditional dances that most weddings had. No one seemed to notice.

"Dance with me."

I looked up sharply at him.

"You don't waltz."

"Come on," he said, taking my hand and pulling me toward the dance floor. "Give me a whirl."

"Christopher. You don't have to..."

But then I was in his arms and we were dancing. Waltzing.

"When did you—?"

"You have to remember, my love. I work for the Worthington family. They can make anything happen."

He took me in for a dip.

"I'm very impressed."

"Turns out I'm a fast learner."

"I guess you are."

Christopher took me around the dance floor.

"Why didn't you tell me?" I asked. "I would have danced with you earlier. I would have let them put it on the program."

"I wanted to surprise you at the right time," he said. "When it was just you and me."

I glanced around. He was right. No one else seemed to notice, except, of course, the photographers. But otherwise, our dance went unnoticed.

"You always surprise me," I said.

"In a good way I hope," he said.

I smiled at this man who was now my husband.

"Always in a good way."

He'd done so many things in the short time that we'd known each other. He'd learned to waltz so he could dance at our wedding. And, even though he had vowed to never buy a car, he had bought a car just so he could drive from Houston to Maple Creek to spend time with me.

We didn't have everything about our future lives figured out, but we would. We would figure it out. Right now all we knew and all we needed to know was that we wanted to be together.

Everything else would fall into place.

"Have I told you how beautiful you look tonight?" he asked as he deftly led me around other dancing couples.

"Hmm. I think you might have."

"Well. I'm certain I haven't told you nearly enough. You're the most beautiful bride I've ever seen."

"Have you seen a lot of brides?" I asked.

"A half dozen. A dozen at most. Enough."

"Then I take that as a compliment."

"A most sincere one. I think your grandmother is looking for us."

"Why?" I asked.

"I don't know. Why don't we go see? And we'll get some cold water."

He led me from the dance floor, asked one of the servers to bring us water, and led us toward my grandmother.

Grandma was standing next to Mr. and Mrs. Worthington.

"Your lessons paid off handsomely," Mr. Worthington said.

"Thank you, Sir."

"You should have told us," Grandma said.

"I wanted it to be a surprise."

"And it was," Grandma said. "We have a surprise for you two, also."

"So many surprises," I said.

"A girl only gets married once," Mrs. Worthington said. "You can't have too many good surprises on your wedding day."

"You're very kind," I said.

"We know you don't have plans for your honeymoon," Grandma said. "So we planned it for you."

"You didn't have to do that," Christopher said, glancing at me.

We hadn't told anyone, but we had rented a cabin in the mountains not far from his sister's house.

She wasn't at the wedding due to travel restrictions from her pregnancy so we were planning to spend some time with her.

Mr. Worthington reached into his tuxedo pocket and pulled out an envelope. Handed it to Christopher.

"You're under no obligation to use them," he said. "But we wanted you to have the option."

"What is it?" I asked, holding Christopher's arm as he opened the envelope.

"Tickets," Christopher said. "to Paris. And a debit card."

"Paris." I looked to Mr. Worthington, Mrs. Worthington, and finally my grandmother. "You didn't have to do this."

"We sent your brother to Paris for his honeymoon," Grandma said. "It only seemed fair that you get to go as well."

"Your sister," I said to Christopher.

"She'll understand. We'll go there when we get back."

Paris! I grinned and hugged my grandmother, then Mr. Worthington and Mrs. Worthington.

"This is so unexpected. And so wonderful. How do we thank you?"

"You go," Mrs. Worthington said. "And you have a wonderful time. Don't worry about anything."

"We can do that," Christopher said, pulling me into a hug and kissing me on the lips.

Then he looked to the three older ones. My grandmother and Mr. and Mrs. Worthington who had become like grandparents to him.

"Will you excuse us?" he asked. "I'd like to take my wife for a dance around the room."

As Christopher took my arm, I heard Mr. Worthington whisper something to Mrs. Worthington.

"We did it again, my love."

I didn't hear her answer, but whatever it was, it made no sense to me.

Christopher swept me around the room into a waltz.

I didn't need a fancy wedding or a fancy honeymoon.

Those were things that just came with the territory.

All I needed was the man with his arms wrapped around me, sweeping me around the room.

I'd taken a chance on a stranger.

And now my life was perfect.

Just like the fairy tales.

Keep Reading for a preview of *Accidentally Forever*...

KATHRYN KALEIGH

Accidentally Forever

THE ASHTONS
FOREVER AND EVER

Chapter 1
Grace Miller

JUST ONE MORE PATIENT and I could call it a day.

I sat at my desk with my back to the window. On purpose. Too many distractions to try to work facing the window. I usually even lowered the shades when patients were in my office.

This fifth floor office had a clear view of the 610 West Loop looking out toward River Oaks. I couldn't see downtown Houston from here, but if I went up on the roof I could. From here downtown was so far away, it looked like a tiny cluster of buildings. Something a child might have built out of blocks.

No one went on the roof this time of year. Full on August in Houston was not the time for taking a break on the roof even if it had nice seating to enjoy the nice view. The building managers were talking about making the rooftop a green space with orange trees, but so far no one had moved in that direction.

Slipping my heels off, I rested my bare feet on the tops of my shoes. I wore what I considered appropriately conservative work attire. A dark gray pencil skirt with a matching blazer that hit at my waist. A white collared shirt. And of course, my heels.

I dragged the comb out of my hair and let my long hair swirl around my shoulders as I stretched my arms and got the blood flowing.

I had one hour to sit at my desk and catch up on notes for the day. I opened up my laptop and logged into the charting program my business partner insisted we use.

Me? I was okay with notes typed into a Word document and printed out supplemented by my handwritten notes neatly filed in folders and kept in a locked filing cabinet. A system that had served me well for the two years I'd had my own practice.

But going in with Jonathan had been a smart business move. He had more experience which meant he had more patients and not just that. He was on staff with the mental hospital and got frequent referrals. More than he could handle.

That's where I came in. I'd been with Jonathan for three months now and I was steadily building my patient load. At the rate I was going, Jonathan was going to have to bring in another psychologist before long.

He would have to lease another office if he did that and probably hire a receptionist. I had his old office and he had taken an empty larger one down the hall. There wasn't really space for a receptionist, but he would figure it out.

I was already working late at least three nights a week, one of them being tonight. I had to decide if I wanted to add Saturdays or another late night.

The office space was in a recently renovated building with freshly painted walls and hardwood floors. Very clean. Very modern.

I tried to make sure my space wasn't intimidating. I kept a cinnamon and vanilla candle lit and fresh flowers, currently white daisies, on the corner of my desk. I personally preferred the scent of daffodils, but the florist had been out when I'd stopped by this morning. Daisies were fine though.

This side of the office was what I considered the working side. Desk and a small bookcase with books I used often including the DSM.

The other side of the office was the therapeutic side. Two comfortable chairs and a love seat. One of the chairs was mine. I let the patients choose whether they wanted to sit on the sofa or the other chair.

No coffee table between us. Just a big bookcase with books that were more likely to appeal to patients. Self-help books, mostly. A strong believer in bibliotherapy, I kept it well stocked with my favorite books that I tended to give away.

All part of the cost of doing business.

I was fairly fast at charting, so I was well into my last patient's notes when my phone alarm went off, reminding me to get ready for my seven o'clock patient.

All I knew about him was that he was a twenty-seven-year-old male. I usually had a diagnosis when they were referrals from the hospital, but this man had self-referred through our website.

I saved everything on the computer, logged out, and got ready for my patient. A cold bottle of water on the end table for the client.

A new client intake form for me. It was just a habit to have it with me. I never looked at the intake sheets anymore. I had all the questions memorized and I was good at remembering what we talked about.

When the elevator opened, I glanced at the clock on the wall. My patient was five minutes early. I took this as a good sign.

Since people tended to get turned around coming off the elevator, I went to the door.

This man, however, was walking right toward my office.

Maybe walking wasn't quite the right word. Sauntering was a more accurate word.

Tall and lean, he was handsome with a sexy five-o'clock shadow that many men would envy.

As he sauntered toward me, pulling off aviator sunglasses as he walked, he struck a feminine chord deep down in my reptilian brain. I recognized the way my heart rate sped up and butterflies took flight in my stomach.

He's a patient.

I tamped down those primitive feelings of attraction and gave him my most professional smile.

In the process of tamping down my attraction, I felt myself leaning toward the other end of the spectrum. Extremely professional.

"Come in," I said. "Have a seat."

Chapter 2
Benjamin Ashton

I VALETED my rental car at my buddy Jonathan's office building and headed straight for the fifth floor.

I could have taken an Uber from the airport, but sometimes I just liked the challenge of navigating city traffic on a busy freeway.

Since I had been here when Jonathan moved into this office building, I was more than familiar with the layout.

The spacious lobby with tall ceilings and bright chandeliers would be intimidating to a lot of people, but Jonathan—Dr. Jonathan Baker—didn't worry about such things. He was going for the high-end clients and did so unabashedly. Ambition was his middle name and from what I could tell, he was doing quite well in that direction.

The building had tall imposing live green plants placed strategically around as well as oversized furniture where people could wait for their appointments or just sit and use the WIFI.

The building held all sorts of professional offices. It had a psychiatrist, a chiropractor, a whole floor for attorneys, and a floor for some kind of stock trading.

The rent in this place alone required a certain level of clients. Apparently Jonathan knew what he was doing. The last time I talked to him—about six months ago, maybe longer—he'd been talking about expanding his business. Hiring on some help.

Not a bad idea, but I recommended he put an attorney on retainer.

Not only did I come from a family of entrepreneurs located in Pittsburgh, but I worked for Noah Worthington of Skye Travels. Skye Travels was the premier private airline company in the country.

Noah had taken one small airplane and built a billion dollar company on his own. He was a legend in the field of aviation. New graduates lined up at his door to be interviewed. I was no exception.

I'd been lucky. He'd branched out to Pittsburgh, and was looking to hire a pilot for there.

Long story, but it was around that same time that I learned that Noah Worthington was actually my grandfather's brother.

So he was Uncle Noah. An odd turn of events that had turned out well. The two brothers had gotten reacquainted after having lost touch with each other for most of their adult lives.

It was hard to think of him as Uncle Noah. Instead, I mostly thought of him as the boss.

At any rate, I knew a little bit about starting and running a business.

The elevator that took me up to the fifth floor had that fresh clean scent that smelled like success.

I should have called him. He often worked late, doing paperwork, but it was possible he had a client at this late hour. It was okay. I didn't mind waiting.

I stepped off the elevator into a wide carpeted hallway and headed straight for his office. Realizing I still wore my sun glasses, I pulled them off and blinked as my eyes adjusted.

I nearly came to a stop and would have except that my feet had unstoppable momentum.

A young lady stood at Jonathan's door. Maybe he'd hired some help already.

"Come on in," she said. "Have a seat."

Not one to argue with a pretty girl, I did as she asked.

She was a petite thing, even in high heels, dressed in a professional skirt and blazer.

Professional down to the white collared shirt.

I followed her inside the office. I recognized the view and although the office had the same general arrangement, things looked different.

The couch was new. One of the chairs. White daisies on a vase on the desk. A candle throwing out a mixture of vanilla and cinnamon scent.

Definitely different from Jonathan's décor.

I decided to try out the couch.

She sat across from me, leaning forward, holding a clipboard on her lap.

"I'm pleased that you came in," she said.

"Me too."

"I'd like to start with some basic questions. Then we can see if we're a good match and set up a plan of treatment."

A good match, huh? That was one part I was feeling confident about. As far as a plan of treatment, that sounded a little out of my league.

I glanced over my shoulder.

"I was expecting Jonathan to be here."

"He and I work together," she said. He's just down the hall. Since he's booked ahead several weeks, I was hoping you would give me a chance to work with you."

I realized right then that I was at one of those crossroads that could be life-altering.

The sensation was a little like flying an airplane. I made decisions every day that I hoped led to the best outcome. I had learned to go with my instinct and not second-guess myself. It had served me well so far.

"Okay," I said, giving her a little smile.

"I should introduce myself. I'm Dr. Grace Miller."

I was headed down that slippery slope and although there was still time to jump off, I was intrigued enough to play along.

"Benjamin Ashton."

A brief flash of confusion flashed across her face, but was quickly gone. She didn't recognize my name.

"I don't know much about you," she said. "Your application answers didn't go much further than you being twenty-seven."

"I like my privacy," I said.

Since I was playing along, I decided to be as truthful as I could.

"I understand. So do I. I have just some basic questions to get out of the way. Questions that will help me get to know you better."

"Go ahead," I leaned back, getting comfortable, and stretched one arm out across the back of the couch.

I'd been on a lot of dates. Usually getting to know each other was a little more subtle. Maybe this was a better, more straightforward way to get acquainted.

"Let's start with your occupation."

"I'm a pilot," I said.

"I see. A commercial pilot?"

"I work for a private airline company based here in town."

"Skye Travels?" she asked.

"Is there any other?" I asked with a smile.

"Not that I'm aware of. Do you have any siblings?"

She hadn't so much as glanced at the clipboard in her lap.

"I have two older sisters, one older brother, and one younger brother."

"You have a really big family. What was that like for you? Growing up?"

"I had a good childhood. Our parents were strict, but fair."

"You were close to your siblings?"

"Mostly my younger brother, but we were all close."

"What about now?"

"Now?" I ran a hand along my chin. "Now they're all married."

"And you? Are you married?"

"I'm single."

She didn't even miss a beat. Talking to her reminded me in some ways of having a conversation with Jonathan. He was persistent also. Persistent and straightforward.

"What's it like being the only single person in your family?"

"They're all happy."

She leaned forward, looking into my eyes. Her eyes were a lovely shade of green. The color of a meadow seen from ten thousand feet in the bright sunshine of spring.

Her red bow shaped lips parted slightly, curved into a little smile that she seemed to be fighting a losing battle with. I could tell she was trying, rather unsuccessfully, not to smile.

"But what about you? What's it like for you?"

I shrugged.

"I now have two more sisters and two more brothers."

"You're close to your in-laws."

"We're all close. We all spend a lot of time together."

I opened my mouth to tell her that we all lived in the same house, but closed it. It wasn't something I told people quite simply because it was one of those things that was hard for people to understand.

It was hard for people to understand that our house was large enough to comfortably hold six families. Most people didn't even call it a house. They called it a manor—which it was.

I also didn't tell people that we had a cook, a gardener, and a housekeeper and all of them lived on the grounds.

Those were things I kept to myself.

"Tell me about your parents."

"They worked a lot, still do, but they always had time for us."

"They were supportive of your decision to become a pilot?"

I looked blankly at her a moment, then cleared my throat.

That was the other thing I didn't tell people. Not only did my uncle own the airline, but both of my brothers and both of my brothers-in-law were pilots.

"Yes," I said. "They are very supportive."

I was finding this conversation difficult. It was hard talking to her without telling her everything.

And even though there were things I didn't go around telling people, I wanted to tell her everything.

Chapter 3
Grace

WITH THE CITY ambiance that even drawn shades couldn't block out, I studied my new client.

I wanted to go back to my computer. I was decent at remembering names. I'd had it in my head that his name was Bradford... something. Not Benjamin. Maybe I'd read it wrong. But no. I distinctly remembered making a folder in the computer program with the name Bradford... something.

I'd straighten that out later. Couldn't very well jump up in the middle of a session to go to my computer because I was confused on his name.

So far I didn't see anything that would guide me toward a diagnosis. Jonathan would probably say he was enmeshed with his family, but I believed that to be a good thing. Families these days were too scattered and family support was one of those fundamental things that, in my experience, everyone needed.

When patients had family support, unless those families were completely dysfunctional, they typically fared much better than those who didn't have family support.

I had enough history from him for now. It was time to get some more pertinent information.

"Have you ever been hospitalized for mental health reasons?"

"No," he said.

"Have you ever had any kind of counseling?"

"No."

"You didn't indicate on your contact information anything that you might want to work on. Is there anything in particular that you'd like to talk about?"

He didn't answer right away. I gave him time to think. It was one of those thirty second pauses that seemed to last forever.

"It's just nice to have someone who listens."

If there was anything diagnosable about him, it was going to take some time to get him to talk about it. Private people were usually like that.

"It's hard for you to trust people," I said.

"I don't know if I'd go that far."

"But you don't have anyone you're comfortable talking to."

"I have a good friend. I talk to him."

"Yeah? When is the last time you spoke to him?"

"Christmas, I think. Maybe New Year's."

"So it's been about six months?"

"I guess so."

I wasn't concerned with that. It was typical guy behavior. Guys could go years without talking and still consider themselves good friends. When they picked up the phone, they just picked up the conversation like they had spoken last week.

It wasn't usually like that for women. I didn't like to generalize, but I saw it all the time. In order for girlfriends to remain girlfriends, they had to keep up with each other on a regular basis. Weekly. Sometimes even daily.

I had one friend, but he was a guy—also a graduate student.

Graduate school, then working didn't allow a lot of time for hanging out with friends.

The only people I'd gone out with socially during graduate school was fellow graduate students and all we talked about was psychology.

So I was in no place to judge Benjamin for going six months without talking to his best friend.

"What kinds of things do you do for fun?"

"I fly airplanes."

He said it without hesitation.

"I mean outside of your job."

"Occasional family time. A movie here and there. Grilling outside on family days."

"So no hobbies?"

"Flying is my hobby and my career."

"It's who you are."

"Yes." He sounded surprised that I understood that.

I knew what it was like to eat, sleep, and breathe one's career. It was what it took.

Having a career like psychology or aviation took complete focus.

My watch vibrated, telling me that we only had ten minutes left in the session.

"We only have about ten minutes left," I said. "So I'd like to go over what we talked about."

"Okay. Sure." He leaned forward and looked into my eyes. His eyes were a lovely deep cerulean blue that a girl could fall into.

How was it that a guy like this was still single?

Maybe that was something he wanted to work on.

"You're a pilot for Skye Travels. Flying is your passion. The one thing that's a constant in your life.

"You're close to your family. Two brothers, one older, one younger, and two older sisters. They're all married and you like their spouses. Am I right so far?"

"Impressively so."

"You have good family support and a good friend that you can talk to about just about anything. You're here because you just want someone to talk to."

"Yes," he said.

"Does this time and day work for you?"

He looked away for a moment. Gave me another one of those thirty second forever silences.

"I have an erratic schedule. I never know where I'll be."

"I can see where having someone to talk to could be a problem. Why don't you use the scheduling feature on the website to schedule your next session yourself. I'll recognize your name and I'll know you aren't a new client. Does that sound good to you?"

"It sounds okay to me," he said.

"So. Our time is up for now. Is there anything you'd like to add before you go?"

Clients invariably saved their true reason for coming to therapy for the last five minutes of the session. I always braced myself when I asked that question. I knew of psychologists had stopped asking for that very reason.

"Nothing to add," he said. "I enjoyed talking to you."

"Likewise."

He stood up from the couch and I stood up with him, holding my clipboard with both hands at my waist.

"Until next week then," he said.

"Next week. Whenever works for you."

"I'll let you know when I'm back in town."

"Take care, Benjamin," I said, walked to the door, and opened it.

"Good night," he said.

After stepping out into the hallway, I went back to my computer. I wanted to double-check his name. It wasn't like me to get the name of a new client wrong.

I went straight to the computer and logged in.

Ah ha. I had been right.

My client's name was Bradford.

And Bradford had sent an email asking to reschedule.

Chapter 4
Benjamin

I CHECKED my watch as I stepped out of Dr. Miller's office.

I'd been in her office for fifty minutes, but it didn't seem like it. It seemed like I'd been there for about fifteen minutes. Time had flown by.

I stood in the hallway and considered. Jonathan had obviously moved his office. And he had obviously added someone into his fold. Just as he had said he would.

The problem at the moment was that I didn't know where to find Jonathan.

I walked to the end of the hall, checking names on doors as I went.

And there at the end of the hallway, I found his name on the door.

Dr. Jonathan Baker.

Since his door was closed, I sent him a text.

> Hey. I'm outside your new office.

He wouldn't answer if he was with a patient.

But he answered right back.

JONATHAN

I'm at the bar downstairs.

This day was just getting stranger and stranger.

> Do you want company?

JONATHAN

Sure. Come down.

Going back the way I came, I passed by Dr. Grace Miller's closed office. I was still a little dazed by that whole experience.

I had just gone through an entire counseling session.

I stopped, my hand almost to the elevator button.

Well hell.

I had just taken up an hour of her time that had been reserved for someone else.

That hardly seemed right.

I had to pay her for her time. For me the hour had been a casual interesting interlude, but for her, it had been work.

I never carried cash anymore, but I did keep one check on me for emergencies. I still, in this modern day and age, occasionally encountered someone who did not take credit cards, but oddly enough, would take a check.

Tugging the folded check out of my wallet, I wrote it out to her, leaving the amount blank, and signed it.

I wrote a note on the back.

I know I wasn't your scheduled client. Please fill in your rate for new clients.

I hesitated. I was running out of room, but I had so much I wanted to say. I boiled it down to the gist of it all.

Thank you for listening.

Feeling much better, I slid the check underneath her door and went straight to the elevator.

Maybe I'd have just one beer with Jonathan. It was early and I didn't have another flight until in the morning.

I needed to figure out just how much I was going to tell him about my hour with Dr. Miller.

Nothing. That's what I was going to tell him.

He'd probably tell me it was unethical pretending to be a client when I wasn't.

It wouldn't matter, or maybe it would make matters even worse, that I had enjoyed talking to Grace.

I got off the elevator, went outside, and walked across the street to the little bar where he and I had spent quite a few hours in our younger days. These days it wasn't like Jonathan to be here. He was typically home with his wife if he wasn't working.

But then again, as I had admitted to Grace, it had been six months since I had spoken to him. I had no way of knowing what was going on in his life right now.

He and I needed to do a better job of keeping up with each other.

I stepped into the upscale bar called simply *Equinox* and looked around for Jonathan.

The bar, a favorite hangout for the after work crowd was loud and the servers were hopping.

Jonathan, seeing me walk in, held up a hand and I spotted him across the room.

I slid into the booth across from him.

"What are you doing here?" I asked. "Why aren't you with Victoria?"

"Victoria left me."

Keep Reading *Accidentally Forever*...

Kathryn Kaleigh writes sweet contemporary romance, time travel romance, and historical romance.

kathrynkaleigh.com

9 798330 384549